PLOTTING IN PIRATE SEAS

Francis Rolt-Wheeler

CONTENTS

American All Through

The tom-tom throbbed menacingly through the heavy dark of the Haitian night.

Under its monotonous and maddening beat, Stuart Garfield moved restlessly.

Why had his father not come back? What mystery lay behind?

Often though the boy had visited the island, he had never been able to escape a sensation of fear at that summons of the devotees of Voodoo. Tonight, with the mysterious disappearance of his father weighing heavily on his spirits, the roll of the black goatskin drum seemed to mock him.

Hippolyte, the giant negro who had been their guide into this back-country jungle, rocked and grimaced in balance with the rhythm.

"Why are they beating that drum, Hippolyte?" demanded Stuart, suddenly.

"Tonight the night of the Full Moon, Yes," was the answer. "Always Voodoo feast that night. Often, queer things happen on night of Full Moon, Yes!"

Stuart turned impatiently to the door, as much to get his eyes away from the hypnotic swaying of Hippolyte as to resume his watch for his father. The negro's reference to "queer things" had added to the boy's uneasiness.

Little though Stuart knew about his father's affairs, he was aware that his investigations dealt with matters of grave importance to the United States. Ever since Mr. Garfield had resigned his position in the U. S. Consular Service and left the post in Cuba, where he had stayed so many years, he had kept a keen eye on international movements in the West Indies.

Mr. Garfield was an ardent and flaming patriot. He believed the Monroe Doctrine with a conviction that nothing could shake. He regarded all the islands of the West Indies as properly under the sheltering wing of the United States. He looked with unfriendly eye upon the possession of certain of the islands by England, France and Holland, and especially distrusted the colonies of European powers upon South American and Central American shores.

Stuart was even more intense in his patriotism. He had not lived in the United States since early childhood, and saw the country of the Stars and Stripes enhaloed by romance.

Though Stuart had been brought up in Cuba, all his tastes ran to things American. He had learned to play pelota, and was a fair player, but the rare occasions when he could get a game of baseball suited him far better. He cared nothing for books unless they dealt with the United States, and then he read with avidity. Western stories fired his imagination, the more so because the life they described was so different from his own.

Stuart was not the type of boy always seeking a fight, but, beneath his somewhat gentle brown eyes and dark hair, there was a square aggressive chin, revealing that trait of character known as a "terrible finisher." It took a good deal to start Stuart, but he was a terror, once started. Any criticism of the United States was enough to get him going. His Cuban schoolmates had found that out, and, whenever Stuart was around, the letters "U. S." were treated with respect.

This square chin was aggressively thrust forward now, as the boy looked into the night. There was trouble in the air. He felt it. Deeper down than the disturbed feelings produced by the tom-tom, he sensed a prescience of evil on its way.

When, therefore, a figure emerged from the forest into the clearing, and Stuart saw that this figure was not his father, but that of a negro, the boy stiffened himself.

"You—Stuart?" the newcomer queried.

"Yes," replied the boy, "that's my name."

The negro hardly hesitated. He walked on, though Stuart was full in the doorway, jostled him aside roughly, and entered. This attitude toward the white man, unheard of anywhere else, is common in up-country Haiti, where, for a century, the black man has ruled, and where the white man is hated and despised.

A hard stone-like gleam came into Stuart's eyes, but even his mounting rage did not blind him to the fact that the negro was twice his size and three times as muscular. Nor did he forget that Hippolyte was in the hut, and, in any case of trouble, the two blacks would combine against him.

The negro who had pushed him aside paid no further attention to the boy, but entered into a rapid-fire conversation with Hippolyte. Stuart could follow the Haitian French dialect quite well, but there were so many half-hidden allusions in the speech of the two men that it was easy for him to see that they were both members of some secret band.

The intruder was evidently in some authority over Hippolyte, for he concluded:

"Everything is well, Yes. Do with the boy, as was arranged."

So saying, he cast a look at Stuart, grinned evilly, and left the hut. The boy watched him until his powerful figure was lost to view in the forest.

Then he turned to Hippolyte.

"What does all this mean!" he demanded, as authoritatively as he could.

For a moment Hippolyte did not answer. He looked at the boy with a reflection of the same evil grin with which the other had favored the white boy.

A quick choke came into the boy's throat at the change in the negro's manner. He was in Hippolyte's power, and he knew it. But he showed never a quiver of fear as he faced the negro.

"What does it all mean?" he repeated.

"It is that you know Manuel Polliovo?"

Stuart knew the name well. His father had mentioned it as that of a conspirator who was in some way active in a West Indian plot.

"I have heard of him," the boy answered.

"Manuel—he send a message, Yes. He say—Tell Stuart he must go away from Haiti, at once. His father gone already."

"What does that mean!" exclaimed Stuart. The first words of the warning had frightened him, but, with the knowledge that his father was in danger, the fighting self of him rose to the surface, and his fear passed.

"How?" returned the negro, not understanding.

"That my father has gone already?"

Hippolyte shrugged his shoulders with that exaggeration of the French shrug common in the islands.

"Maybe Manuel killed him," came the cheerful suggestion. "Jules, who tell me just now, says Manuel, he have the air very wicked and very pleased when he tell him."

Stuart doubted this possibility. Ever since the American occupation of Haiti, in 1915, murder had become less common. The boy thought it more likely that the missing man had been captured and imprisoned. But just what could Manuel be doing if he dared such drastic action? The lad wished that he knew a little more about his father's plans.

A small revolver was in his pocket, and, for one wild moment, Stuart thought of making a fight for it and going to the rescue of his father. But his better sense prevailed. Even supposing he could get the drop on the negro—which was by no means sure—he could not mount guard on him perpetually. Moreover, if he got near enough to try and tie him up, one sweep of those brawny arms would render him powerless.

"And if I do not go?" he asked.

"But you do go," declared Hippolyte. "It is I who will see to that, Yes!"

"Was it Manuel who sent you the money?"

"Ah, the good money!" The negro showed his teeth in a wide grin. "Manuel, he tell Jules to find boy named Stuart. If you big, tie you and take you to the forest; if little, send you away from the island."

This was one point gained, thought Stuart. Manuel, at least, did not know what he looked like.

"I suppose I've got to go to Cap Haitien."

"But, Yes."

"And when?"

"But now, Yes!"

"It's a long walk," protested Stuart. "Twenty miles or more."

"We not walk, No! Get mules near. Now, we start."

The boy had hoped, in some way, to get the negro out of the hut and to make a bolt for the woods where he might lie hidden, but this sudden action prevented any such ruse. He turned to the table to put into his knapsack the couple of changes of clothing he had brought. There was no way for him to take his father's clothes, but the boy opened the larger knapsack and took all the papers and documents.

"See here, Hippolyte," he said. "I give you all these clothes. I take the papers."

The negro grinned a white-toothed smile at the gift. He cared nothing about the papers. He would do what Jules had paid him to do, and no more.

As they left the hut, it seemed to Stuart that the nerve-racking beating of the tom-tom sounded louder and nearer. They walked a mile or so, then, as Hippolyte suggested, at a small half-abandoned plantation, they found mules. Once mounted, the negro set off at break-neck speed, caring nothing about the roughness of the road, all the more treacherous because of the dead-black of the shadows against the vivid green-silver patches where the tropical moonlight shone through.

"What's the hurry?" clamored Stuart, who could see no reason for this mad and reckless riding.

"The dance stop at dawn! I want to be back, Yes!"

They galloped on as before.

A few miles from the town, Stuart snatched at an idea which flashed upon him suddenly.

"Hippolyte," he said. "You want to get back for the voodoo dance?"

"But, Yes!"

"You'll be too late if you take me into town. See."

He showed his watch and held out a twenty-five gourde bill.

"Suppose I give you this. It's all the money I have. You can tell Jules to tell Manuel that you saw me get on board a steamer in Cap Haitien, and that you saw the steamer start. Then you can be back in plenty of time for the dance."

Hippolyte hesitated. The temptation was strong.

"Unless, of course," the boy added carelessly, "you like this white man, Manuel, so much."

An expression of primitive hate wrote itself on the ebon face, a peculiarly malignant snarl, as seen by moonlight.

"I hate all whites!" he flashed.

"Then why should you do a good turn for this Manuel?"

The instincts of a simple honesty struggled with the black's desire. A passing gust of wind brought the rhythmic beating of the tom-tom clearer to their ears. It was the one call that the jungle blood of the negro could not resist. He held out his hand for the money.

"You go into Cap Haitien alone?" he queried, thickly.

"Yes, I'll promise that," the boy agreed.

He dismounted, swung his knapsack on his back, and handed the reins of the mule to Hippolyte, who sat, still uncertain. But the negro's head was turned so that he could hear the throbbing of the drum, and, with an answering howl that went back to the days of the African jungle, he turned and sped back over the rough trail at the same headlong speed he had come.

"If he doesn't break his neck!" commented Stuart, as he saw him go, "it'll be a wonder!"

There were yet a couple of hours before dawn, and Stuart plodded along the trail, which could lead to no other place than Cap Haitien. He walked as fast as he could, hoping to reach the city before daylight, but the first streaks of dawn found him still nearly two miles from the town. He did not want to enter the town afoot by daylight. That would be too conspicuous, and there were plans germinating in the boy's head which needed secrecy. He must hide all day, and get into Cap Haitien the next night.

Stuart slipped off the road and wriggled his way through the dense thicket, seeking a place where there was light enough to read, and yet where the foliage was dense enough to prevent him being seen by anyone passing that way.

A few moments' search only were required before he found the ideal spot, and he threw himself down on a pile of leaves with great zest. That mule had been hard riding.

"First of all," he said to himself, half aloud, "I've got to find out where I'm at. Then I'll maybe be able to figure out what I ought to do."

Stuart's mind was not so quick as it was strong. He was a straight up-and-down honest type of fellow, and thoroughly disliked the crafty and intriguing boy or man. He began cautiously, but got warmed up as he went on, and made a whirlwind finish.

It was characteristic of him, thus, not to plunge into any wild and desperate attempt to rescue his father, until he had time to puzzle out the situation and work out a plan of action. He began by reading all the papers and documents he had taken from his father's knapsack. This was a long job, for the papers were full of allusions to subjects he did not understand. It was nearly noon before he had digested them.

Then he lay on his back and looked up through the tracery of leaves overhead, talking aloud so that the sound of his own voice might make his discoveries clearer.

"The way I get it," he mused, "Father's on the trail of some plot against the United States. This plot is breaking loose, here, in Haiti. This Manuel Polliovo's in it, and so is a negro General, Cesar Leborge. There's a third, but the papers don't say who he is.

"Now," he went on, "I've two things to do. I've got to find Father and I've got to find out this plot. Which comes first?"

He rolled over and consulted one or two of the papers.

"Looks like something big," he muttered, kicking his heels meditatively. "I wonder what Father would say I ought to do?"

At the thought, he whirled over and up into a sitting posture.

"If it's dangerous to the U. S.," he said, "that's got to come first. And I don't worry about Father. He can get out of any fix without me."

The glow of his deep-hearted patriotism began to burn in the boy's eyes. He sat rigid, his whole body concentrated in thought.

"If Manuel Polliovo has captured Father," he said aloud, at last, "it must have been because Father was shadowing him. That means that Manuel doesn't want to be shadowed. That means I've got to shadow him. But how?"

The problem was not an easy one. It was obvious that Stuart could not sleuth this Cuban, Manuel, without an instant guess being made of his identity, for white boys were rare in Haiti. If only he were not white. If only——

Stuart thumped on the ground in his excitement.

Why could he not stain his skin coffee-color, like a Haitian boy? If sufficiently ragged, he might be able to pass without suspicion. It might be only for a day or two, for Stuart was sure that his father would appear again on the scene very soon.

This much, at least, he had decided. No one was going to plot against his country if he could help it. There was not much that he could do, but at least he could shadow one of the conspirators, and what he found out might be useful to his father.

This determination reached, the boy hunted for some wild fruit to stay his appetite—he had nothing to eat since the night before—and settled down for the rest of the afternoon to try and dig out the meaning of his father's papers, some of which seemed so clear, while to others he had no clew. It was characteristic of the boy that, once this idea of menace to the United States had got into his head, the thought of personal danger never crossed his mind. The slightly built boy, small even for his age, the first sight of whom would have suggested a serious high-school student rather than a sleuth, possessed the cool ferocity of a ferret when that one love—his love of country—was aroused.

His first step was clear. As soon as it was dark enough to cover his movements, he would go to the house of one of his father's friends, a little place built among the ruins of Cap Haitien, where they had stayed two or three times before. From references in some of the letters, Stuart gathered that his father had confidence in this man, though he was a Haitian negro.

As soon as the shadows grew deep enough, Stuart made his way through the half-grown jungle foliage—the place had been a prosperous plantation during French occupation—and, a couple of hours later, using by-paths and avoiding the town, he came to this negro's house. He tapped at the same window on which his father had tapped, when they had come to Cap Haitien a week or so before, and Leon, the negro, opened the door.

"But, it is you, Yes!" he cried, using the Haitian idiom with its perpetual recurrence of "Yes" and "No," and went on, "and where is Monsieur your father?"

"I don't know," answered Stuart, speaking in English, which he knew Leon understood, though he did not speak it. "I have missed him."

"But where, and but how?" queried Leon, suddenly greatly excited. "Was he already going up to the Citadel?"

Stuart's face flushed with reflected excitement, but his eyes held the negro's steadily. Leon knew more than the boy had expected he would know.

"No," he replied, "I don't think so. I shall have to go."

"It is impossible, impossible, Yes!" cried Leon, throwing up his hands in protest. "I told Monsieur your father that it was impossible for him. And for you—"

A graphic shrug completed the sentence.

Stuart felt a sinking at the pit of his stomach, for he was no braver than most boys. But the twist of his determination held him up.

"Leon," he said, trying to keep his voice steady, though he felt it sounded a little choked, "isn't there the juice of some root which will turn the skin brown, nearly black?"

"But, Yes, the plavac root."

The Haitian peered at the boy.

"You would make yourself a black man?" he continued.

Stuart ignored argument.

"Can you get some? Tonight? Right away?"

"Ah, well; you know—" Leon began.

The boy interrupted him sharply.

"If my father told you to get some, you would get it," he declared peremptorily.

This was a shrewd guess, for, as a matter of fact, there were a number of reasons why Leon should do what Mr. Garfield told him. The negro, who had no means of finding how much or how little the boy knew, shrugged his shoulders hugely, and, with a word of comment, left the house, carrying a lantern. He was back in half an hour with a handful of small plants, having long fibrous roots. These he cut off, placed in a pot, covering them with water, and set the pot on the stove over a slow fire.

"It will not come off the skin as easily as it goes on, No!" he warned.

"Time enough to think about that when I want to take it off," came the boy's reply.

The decoction ready, Leon rubbed it in thoroughly into Stuart's skin. It prickled and smarted a good deal at first, but this feeling of discomfort soon passed away.

"It won't rub off?" queried Stuart.

Leon permitted himself a grim pleasantry.

"Not against a grindstone!"

This positive assertion was as reassuring in one way as it was disquieting in another. Stuart did not want to remain colored for an indefinite period of time. In his heart of hearts he began to wonder if he had not acted a little more hastily, and that if he had asked for Leon's advice instead of ordering him around, he might have found some milder stain. But it was too late to repent or retract now. His skin was a rich coffee brown from head to foot, and his dark eyes and black hair did not give his disguise the lie.

"I'm going to bed," he next announced, "and I want some ragged boy's clothes by morning, Leon. Very ragged. Also an old pair of boots."

"That is not good," protested the Haitian, "every boy here goes barefoot, Yes!"

Stuart was taken aback. This difficulty had not occurred to him. It was true. Not only the boys, but practically nine men out of ten in Haiti go barefoot. This Stuart could not do. Accustomed to wearing shoes, he would cut his feet on the stones at every step he took on the roads, or run thorns into them every step he took in the open country.

"I must have boots," he declared, "but old ones. Those I've been wearing," he nodded to where they lay on the floor—for this conversation was carried on with the boy wearing nothing but his new brown skin—"would give me away at once."

"I will try and get them," answered Leon. His good-humored mouth opened in a wide smile. "Name of a Serpent!" he ejaculated, "but you are the image of the son of my half-sister!"

At which saying, perhaps Stuart ought to have been flattered, since it evidenced the success of his disguise. But, being American, it ruffled him to be told he resembled a negro.

He went to bed, far from pleased with himself and rather convinced that he had been hasty. Yet his last waking thought, if it had been put into words, would have been:

"It's the right thing to do, and I'm going through with it!"

WHERE BLACK MEN RULE

Stuart was not the only person on the streets of Cap Haitien the next morning who was conscious of personal danger. Manuel Polliovo was ill at ease. Bearing the secret that he bore, the Cuban knew that a hint of it would bring him instant death, or, if the authorities had time to intervene, incarceration in a Haitian prison, a fate sometimes worse than death. Even the dreaded presence of U. S. Marines would not hold the negro barbarians back, if they knew.

Manuel was by no means blind to his peril. He was relieved in the thought that the American, Garfield, was where he could not do him any harm, but there were other dangers. Hence he was startled and jumped nervously, on hearing a voice by his elbow.

"Do you want a guide, Senor?"

"A guide, Boy! Where to?"

The answer came clear and meaningly:

"To the Citadel of the Black Emperor!"

The Cuban grew cold, under the burning sun, and, professional conspirator though he was, his face blenched. His hand instinctively sought the pocket wherein lay his revolver.

Yet he dare not kill. Five years of American occupation had bred a sense of law and order in the coast towns, at least, which had not been known in Haiti for a century and more. Any violence would lead to inquiry, and Manuel's record was not one which would bear investigation.

How came this ragged Haitian urchin to know? Manuel's swift glance at Stuart had shown him nothing but a Creole lad in clothes too big for him and a pair of boots fastened with string. The messenger meant nothing, it was the message which held menace.

To the Cuban this apparently chance street encounter was ominous of black threat. It revealed treachery and might mean a trap. But from whence? Swiftly Manuel's keen brain, the brain of an arch-plotter, scanned the manifold aspects of this sudden threat.

How much labor, how many wild adventures, what a series of dangers would Stuart have escaped, had he but been able to read the thoughts of that crafty brain!

Did his fellow-conspirators want to get rid of him? So Manuel's doubts ran. Did they count on his shooting the boy, in a panic, and being lynched for it, there and then, on the street of Cap Haitien? Or of his being imprisoned, tried and executed for murder? Such a plot was not unlikely.

But, if so, who had sent the boy?

Was Cesar Leborge playing him false? True, from that bull-necked, ferocious negro general, Manuel knew he could expect nothing but brutality, envy and hate; but such a design as this boy's intervention seemed too subtle for the giant Creole's brain. Manuel accounted himself master of the negro when it came to treachery and cunning. Moreover, he knew Leborge to be a sullen and suspicious character, little likely to talk or to trust anyone.

What did the boy know? Manuel flashed a look at him. But Stuart was idly fiddling in the dust with the toe of his ragged boot, and the Cuban's suspicions flashed to another quarter.

Could the Englishman, Guy Cecil, be to blame? That did not seem any more likely. Manuel was afraid of Cecil, though he would not admit it, even to himself. The Englishman's chill restraint, even in moments of the most tense excitement, cowed the Cuban. Never had he been able to penetrate into his fellow-conspirator's thoughts. But that Cecil should have talked loosely of so vital, so terrible a secret? No. The grave itself was not more secretive than that quiet schemer, of whom nothing ever seemed to be known. And to a negro boy! No, a thousand times, no!

Stay—was this boy a negro boy? Suspicion changed its seat in the wily Cuban's brain. That point, at least, he would find out, and swiftly. He looked at his ragged questioner, still fiddling with his toe in the dust, and answered.

"Well," he said, "you can show me what there is to be seen in this place. But first I will go to the Café. No," he continued, as the boy turned towards the new part of the town, built under American oversight, "not there. To the Café de l'Opéra. Go down the street and keep a few steps in front."

Stuart obeyed. He had seen the first swift motion of the Cuban's hand, when he had been accosted, and had guessed that it was pistolwards. It was uncomfortable walking in front of a man who was probably aching to blow one's brains out. Nasty little cold shivers ran up and down Stuart's back. But the tents of the U. S. Marines, in camp a little distance down the beach, gave him courage. With his sublime faith in the United States, Stuart could not believe that he could come to any harm within sight of the Stars and Stripes floating from the flagstaff in front of the encampment.

While Stuart was thus getting backbone from his flag, Manuel was concentrating his wits and experience on this problem which threatened him so closely.

Was this boy a negro?

A life spent in international trickery on a large scale had made the Cuban a good judge of men. He knew native races. He knew—what the white man generally ignores or forgets—that between the various black races are mental differences as wide as between races of other color. He knew that the Ewe negro is no more like the Riff in character, than the phlegmatic Dutchman resembles the passionate Italian. If a black, to what race did this boy belong? Was he a black, at all?

The bright sun threw no reflected lights on the boy's skin, the texture of which was darker than that of a mulatto, and had a dead, opaque look, lacking the golden glow of mulatto skin. The lad's hair showed little hint of Bantu ancestry and his feet were small. True, all this might betoken any of the Creole combinations common in Haiti, but the Cuban was not satisfied. If the skin had been stained, now——

"Boy!" he called.

Stuart looked around.

"Here are some coppers for you."

The boy slouched toward him, extended his hand negligently and the Cuban dropped some three-centime pieces into it.

Stuart mumbled some words of thanks, imitating, as far as he could, the Haitian dialect, but, despite his desire to act the part, feeling awkward in receiving charity.

Manuel watched him closely, then, abruptly, bade him go on ahead. The scrutiny had increased his uneasiness.

This self-appointed guide was no negro, no mulatto, of that Manuel was sure. The money had been received without that wide answering grin of pleasure characteristic in almost all negro types. Moreover, the palms of the boy's hands were the same color as the rest of his skin. The Cuban knew well that a certain dirty pallor is always evident on the palms of the hands of even the blackest negroes.

The boy's reference to the "Citadel of the Black Emperor" showed that he was aware of this secret meeting of conspirators.

This was grave.

More, he was disguised.

This was graver still.

Was this boy, too, afraid of Haiti, that savage land at the doors of America; that abode where magic, superstition and even cannibalism still lurk in the forests; that barbarous republic where the white man is despised and hated, and the black man dominates? That land where the only civilizing force for a century has been a handful of American marines!

That this boy was disguised suggested that he was in fear for his life; but, if so, why was he there? How did he come to know the pass-word of the conspiracy? For what mysterious reason did he offer himself as a guide to the haunted place of meeting?

Who was this boy?

Manuel turned into the Café de l'Opéra, a tumble-down frame shack with a corrugated iron roof, to order a cooling drink and to puzzle out this utterly baffling mystery.

The Cuban's first impulse was to flee. Had anything less imperious than this all-important meeting been before him, Manuel would have made his escape without a moment's delay.

Cap Haitien is no place for a white man who has fallen under suspicion. Of the four gateways into Haiti it is the most dangerous. In Jacamal, a white man may be left alone, so long as he does not incur the enmity of the blacks; in Gonaive the foreign holders of concessions may protect him; in Port-au-Prince, the capital, he is safeguarded by the potent arm of the American marines; but, in the country districts back of Cap Haitien, the carrion buzzards may be the only witnesses of his fate. And, to that back country, the Cuban must go. All this, Manuel knew, and he was a shrewd enough man to dare to be afraid.

Stuart squatted in the shadow of the building while the Cuban sipped from his glass. Thus, each doubting the other, and each fearing the other, they gazed over the busy desolation of Cap Haitien, a town unlike any other on earth.

Save for a small and recently rebuilt section in the heart of the town—which boasted some 10,000 inhabitants—flimsy frame houses rose in white poverty upon the ruins of what was once known as "the little Paris of the West Indies." Of the massive buildings of a century ago, not one remained whole. The great earthquake of 1842 did much toward their destruction; the orgy of loot and plunder which followed, did more; but the chiefest of all agents of demolition was the black man's rule.

The spacious residences were never rebuilt, the fallen aqueducts were left in ruins, the boulevards fell into disrepair and guinea-grass rioted through the cracked pavements. Back of the town the plantations were neglected, the great houses fallen, while the present owners lived contentedly in the little huts which once had been built for slaves. The ruthless hands of time, weather and the jungle snatched back "Little Paris," and Cap Haitien became a huddled cluster of pitiful buildings scattered among the rubbish-heaps and walls of a once-beautiful stone-built town.

This appearance of desolation, however, was contradicted by the evidence of commercial activity. The sea-front was a whirl of noise.

The din of toil was terrific. Over the cobblestoned streets came rough carts drawn by four mules—of the smallest race of mules in the world—and these carts clattered down noisily with their loads of coffee-sacks, the drivers shouting as only a Haitian negro can shout. At the wharf, each cart was at once surrounded by a cluster of negroes, each one striving to outshout his fellows, while the bawling of the driver rose high above all. Lines of negroes, naked to the waist, sacks on their glistening backs, poured out from the warehouses like ants from an anthill, but yelling to out-vie the carters. The tiny car-line seemed to exist only to give opportunity for the perpetual clanging of the gong; and the toy wharf railway expended as much steam on its whistle as on its piston-power.

Stuart had visited the southern part of Haiti with his father, especially the towns of Port-au-Prince and Jacamel, and he was struck with the difference in the people. Cap Haitien is a working town and its people are higher grade than the dwellers in the southern part of the republic. The south, however, is more populous. Haiti is thickly inhabited, with 2,500,000 people, of whom only 5,000 are foreigners, and of these, not more than 1,000 are whites. The island is incredibly fertile. A century and a quarter ago it was rich, and could be rich again. Its coffee crop, alone, could bring in ample wealth.

To Stuart's eyes, coffee was everywhere. The carts were loaded with coffee, the sacks the negroes carried were coffee-sacks, the shining green berries were exposed to dry on stretches of sailcloth in vacant lots, among the ruins on the sides of the streets. Haitian coffee is among the best in the world, but the Haitian tax is so high that the product cannot be marketed cheaply, the American public will not pay the high prices it commands, and nearly all the crop is shipped to Europe.

"Look at that coffee!" Stuart's father had exclaimed, just a week before. "Where do you suppose it comes from, Stuart? From cultivated plantations? Very little of it. Most of the crop is picked from half-wild shrubs which are the descendants of the carefully planted and cultivated shrubs which still linger on the plantations established under French rule, a century and a half ago. A hundred years of negro power in Haiti has stamped deterioration, dirt and decay on the island."

"But that'll all change, now we've taken charge of the republic!" had declared Stuart, confident that the golden letters "U. S." would bring about the millennium.

His father had wrinkled his brows in perplexity and doubt.

"It would change, my boy," he said, "if America had a free hand. But she hasn't."

"Why not?"

"Because, officially, we have only stepped in to help the Haitians arrive at 'self-determination.' The treaty calls for our aid for ten years, with a possibility of continuing that protection for another ten years. But we're not running the country, we're only policing it and advising the Haitians as to how things should be handled."

"Do you think they'll learn?"

"To govern themselves, you mean? Yes. To govern themselves in a civilized manner? No. I wouldn't go so far as to say that slavery or peonage are the only ways to make the up-country Haitian negro work, though a good many people who have studied conditions here think so.

"The program of the modern business man in Haiti is different: Make the negro discontented with his primitive way of living, give him a taste for unnecessary luxuries, teach him to envy his neighbor's wealth and covet his neighbor's goods, and then make him work in order to earn the money to gratify these wishes, and civilization will begin.

"Mark you, Stuart, I don't say that I endorse this program, I'm only telling you, in half-a-dozen words, what it really is. It is sure, though, that when the black man rules, he relapses into savagery; when he obeys a white master, he rises toward civilization."

Stuart remembered this, now, as he sat outside the café, and looked pridefully at the tents of the U. S. Marines in the distance. He realized that American improvements in the coast towns had not changed the nature of the Haitian negro, or creole, as he prefers to be called.

Under his father's instruction, the boy had studied Haitian history, and he knew that the Spaniards had ruled by fear, the French had ruled by fear, the negro emperors and presidents had ruled by fear, and, under the direct eye of the U. S. Marines, Haiti is still ruled by fear. In a dim way—for Stuart was too young to have grasped it all—the boy felt that this was not militarism, but the discipline necessary to an undeveloped race.

Only the year before, Stuart himself had been through an experience which brought the innate savagery of the Haitian vividly before his eyes. He had been in Port-au-Prince when the Cacos undertook to raid the town, seize the island, and sweep the United States Marines into the sea. And, as he had heard a Marine officer tell his father, but for a chance accident, they might have succeeded.

In October, 1919, Charlemagne Peralte, the leader of the Cacos, was killed by a small punitive party of U. S. Marines. The Cacos may be described as Haitian patriots or revolutionists, devotees of serpent and voodoo worship, loosely organized into a secret guerilla army. They number at least 100,000 men, probably more. About one-half of the force is armed with modern rifles. The headquarters of the Cacos is in the mountain country in the center of the island, above the Plain of Cul-de-Sac, where no white influence reaches. No one who knew Haitian conditions doubted that revenge would be sought for Charlemagne's death, and all through the winter of 1919-1920, the Marines were on the alert for trouble.

The Cacos leadership had devolved upon Benoit, a highly educated negro, who had secured the alliance of "the Black Pope" and Chu-Chu, the two lieutenants of Charlemagne. Upon Benoit fell the duty of "chasing the white men into the sea" and exterminating the Americans, just as Toussaint l'Ouverture drove the English, and Dessalines, Christophe and Pétion drove the French, a century before.

Nearly four years of American occupation had passed. That the purpose of the United States was purely philanthropic was not—and is not—believed by the vast majority of the Haitians. Though living conditions have improved vastly, though brigandage on the plains has ceased, and though terrorism has diminished, at heart only the Haitian merchants and job-holders like the American occupation. The educated Creoles tolerate it. The semi-savages of the hills resent it.

On January 16, some of the white men in Port-au-Prince noticed that the Creoles were excited and nervous. At the Café Bordeaux, at the Seaside Inn, at the Hotel Bellevue, strange groups met and mysterious passwords were exchanged. Sullen and latent hostility was changing from smouldering rancor to flaming hate. Port-au-Prince was ripe for revolt.

Stuart remembered his father's return that night.

"Son," he had said, putting a revolver on the little table beside his bed, "I hope you won't have to use this, but, at least, I've taught you to shoot straight."

That night, Benoit, gathering up the local detachments of his forces, moved them in scattered groups through the abandoned plantations and off the main roads to the outskirts of the city. He had over 1,800 men with him. Most had modern rifles. All had machetes. All over the island other bands were in readiness, their orders being to wait until they heard of the fall of Port-au-Prince, when the massacre of all whites might begin.

Benoit's plan was to take the city at daybreak. At midnight, he started three columns of 300 men each, from three directions. They wandered into the city by twos and threes, taking up positions. Their orders were, that, at the firing of a gun at daybreak, when the stores opened, they were to rush through the business district, setting fires everywhere and killing the white men and the gendarmerie. Benoit believed that, while his men could not withstand a pitched battle with the Marines, they could sweep the town in guerilla fashion when the Marines were scattered here and there, putting out fires. Moreover, the Cacos general was sure that, once a massacre of the whites was begun, race hatred would put all the black population on his side.

Two o'clock in the morning came. Mr. Elliott, manager of a sugar refinery at Hascoville, a suburb two miles out of the city, was sleepless, and a vague uneasiness possessed him. Thinking that the fresh air might be beneficial, he went to a window and looked out.

"Out of the myriad hissing, rustling and squawking noises of a tropic night, he heard the unmistakable 'chuff-chuff-chuff' of a marching column of barefoot men. He made out a single-file column moving rapidly across a field, off the road. He made out the silhouetes of shouldered rifles. Far off, under a yellow street lamp, he glimpsed a flash of a red shirt. That was enough. He telephoned to the Marine Brigade that the Cacos were about to raid Port-au-Prince.

"Benoit's bubble," continued the report of the Special Correspondent of the New York World, "burst right there. Only about 150 of his 300 'shock troops' had reached the market-place. No fires had been set. The people were all in bed and asleep. There were no materials for a panic.

"The Marines, in patrols and in larger formations, spread through the streets swiftly to the posts arranged for emergency. Leslie Coombs, one of the Marines, saw several men enter the market, where they had no right to be; he ran to the door and was set upon by machete men, who slashed him and cut him down, but not until he had emptied his automatic.

"The shooting and hand-to-hand fighting spread in a flash all through the business part of the city. The rest of the surprise detachment of the

Cacos made a rush for the center of the city. One block was set on fire and burned.

"The Marines deployed steadily and quickly. They put sputtering machine guns on the corners and cleaned the principal streets. There was fighting on every street and alley of a district more than a mile square.

"The Cacos stood their ground bravely for a while, but their case was hopeless. The American fire withered them. First those on the rim of the city, and then those inside, turned their faces to the hills. The main body, realizing that the plan of attack was ruined, started a pell-mell retreat.

"The Marines moved from the center of the city, killing every colored man who was not in the olive-drab uniform of the gendarmerie.

"As the sky turned pink and then flashed into blazing daylight, the fight became a hunt. On every road and trail leading from the city, Marine hunted Cacos.

"One hundred and twenty-two dead Cacos were found in and about the city; bodies found along the line of retreat in the next few days raised the total of known dead to 176. There were numerous prisoners, among them the famous chieftain, Chu-Chu." It was a swift and merciless affair, but, as Stuart's father had commented, no one who knew and understood Haitian conditions denied that it had been well and wisely done.

Stuart had seen some of the fighting, and his father had pointed out to him that Port-au-Prince is not the whole of Haiti, nor does one repulse quell a revolt. The boy knew, and the Cuban, watching him, knew that for every man the Marines had slain, two had joined the Cacos and had sworn the blood-oath before the High Priest and the High Priestess (papaloi and mamaloi) of Voodoo.

Revolt against the American Occupation, therefore, was an ever-present danger. Stuart wondered whether the negro who had been sent to him by Manuel were a Cacos, and, if so, whether his father were a prisoner among the Cacos. Manuel, for his part, wondered who this boy might be, who had darkened his skin in disguise. One thing the Cuban had determined and that was that he would not let the boy know that his disguise had been penetrated. None the less, he must find out, if possible, how the lad had come to know about the meeting-place of the conspirators.

Finishing his drink, the Cuban rose, and, motioning to Stuart to precede him, walked to the sparsely settled section between the commercial center of the town and the Marine encampment. When the shouts of the toiling workers had grown faint in the distance, the Cuban stopped.

"Boy!" he called.

Stuart braced himself. He knew that the moment of his test had come. His heart thumped at his ribs, but he kept his expression from betraying fear. He turned and faced the Cuban.

"In my right-hand pocket," said Manuel, in his soft and languorous voice, "is a revolver. My finger is on the trigger. If you tell one lie—why, that is the end of you! Why did you mention the Citadel of the Black Emperor?"

Stuart's heart gave a bound of relief. He judged, from Manuel's manner, that his disguise had not been guessed. Elated with this supposed success, he commenced to tell glibly the tale he had prepared and studied out the day before.

"I wanted to give you a warning," he said.

The Cuban's gaze deepened.

"Warning? What kind of a warning? From whom?"

"Cesar Leborge," answered Stuart. He had judged from his father's papers that the two were engaged in a conspiracy, and thought that he could do nothing better than to provoke enmity between them. The proverb "When thieves fall out, honest men come by their own," rang through his head.

Manuel was obviously impressed.

"What do you know about this?" he asked curtly. "Tell your story."

"I hate Leborge," declared Stuart, trying to speak as a negro boy would speak. "He took away our land and killed my father. I want to kill him. He never talks to anybody, but he talks to himself. The other night I overheard him saying he 'must get rid of that Cuban at the Citadel of the Black Emperor.'

"So when I saw you here in Cap Haitien, I took a chance on it's being you he meant. If it hadn't been you, my asking you if you wanted a guide wouldn't have been out of the way."

"You are a very clever boy," said Manuel, and turned away to suppress a smile.

Certainly, he thought, this boy was a very clumsy liar. Stuart had never tried to play a part before, and had no natural aptitude for it. His imitation of the Haitian accent was poor, his manner lacked the alternations of arrogance and humility that the Haitian black wears. Then his story of the shadowing of Leborge was not at all in character. And, besides, as the Cuban had convinced himself, the boy was not a Haitian negro at all.

Then, suddenly, a new thought flashed across Manuel's mind. He had thought only of his fellow-conspirators as traitors. But there was one other who had some inkling of the plot—Garfield, the American.

And Garfield had a boy!

The Cuban's lip curled with contempt at the ease with which he had unmasked Stuart. He had only to laugh and announce his discovery, for the boy to be made powerless.

It was a temptation. But Manuel was too wily to yield to a temptation merely because it was pleasurable. As long as the boy did not know that he had been found out, he would live in a Fool's Paradise of his own cleverness. Believing himself unsuspected, he would carry out his plans—whatever they were—the while that Manuel, knowing his secret, could play with him as a cat plays with a mouse she has crippled.

He decided to appear to believe this poorly woven story.

"If you hate Leborge, and Leborge hates me," he said, "I suppose we are both his enemies. I presume," he added, shrewdly, "if I refused to take you with me to the Citadel of the Black Emperor, you would shadow me, and go any way."

A flash of assent came into the boy's eyes, which, he was not quick enough to suppress. Decidedly, Stuart was not cut out for a conspirator, and would never be a match for the Cuban in guile.

"I see you would," the Cuban continued. "Well, I would rather have you within my sight. Here is money. Tomorrow, an hour after sunrise, be at the door of the hotel with the best horses you can find. I wish to be at Millot by evening."

Stuart took the money and preceded Manuel into the town, chuckling inwardly at his cleverness in outwitting this keen conspirator. But he would have been less elated with his success if he had heard the Cuban mutter, as he turned into the porch of the hotel,

"First, the father. Now, the son!"

THE BLOOD-STAINED CITADEL

A foul, slimy ooze, compounded of fat soil, rotting vegetation and verdigris-colored scum, with a fainter green mark meandering through it—such was the road to Millot.

Stuart and the Cuban, the boy riding ahead, were picking their away across this noisome tract of land.

For a few miles out of Cap Haitien, where the finger of American influence had reached, an air of decency and even of prosperity had begun to return. Near the town, the road had been repaired. Fields, long abandoned, showed signs of cultivation, anew.

Two hours' ride out, however, it became evident that the new power had not reached so far. The road had dwindled to a trail of ruts, which staggered hither and thither in an effort to escape the quagmires—which it did not escape. Twice, already, Stuart's horse had been mired and he had to get out of the saddle and half-crawl, half-wriggle on his belly, in the smothering and sucking mud. So far, Manuel had escaped, by the simple device of not passing over any spot which the boy had not tried first.

This caution was not to serve him long, however.

At some sight or sound unnoticed by the rider, Manuel's horse shied from off the narrow path of tussocks on which it was picking its way, and swerved directly into the morass.

The Cuban, unwilling to get into the mud, tried to urge the little horse to get out. Two or three desperate plunges only drove it down deeper and it slipped backward into the clawing mire.

Manuel threw himself from his horse, but he had waited almost too long, and the bog began to draw him down. He was forced to cry for help.

Stuart, turning in his saddle, saw what had happened. He jumped off his horse and ran to help the Cuban. The distance was too great for a hand-clasp. The ragged trousers which Stuart was wearing in his disguise as a Haitian lad were only held up by a piece of string; he had no belt which he could throw. There was no sapling growing near enough to make a stick.

Then there came into the boy's mind an incident in a Western story he had read.

Darting back to his horse, he unfastened the saddle girth, and, hurrying back to where Manuel was floundering in the mud, he threw the saddle outwards, holding the end of the girth. It was just long enough to reach.

With the help of the flat surface given by the saddle and a gradual pulling of the girth by Stuart, the Cuban was at last able to crawl out.

The gallant little horse, freed from its rider's weight, had reached a point where it could be helped, and the two aided the beast to get its forefeet on solid land.

This rescue broke down much of the distance and some of the hostility between Manuel and Stuart, and, as soon as the road began to rise from the quagmire country, and was wide enough to permit it, the Cuban ordered the boy to ride beside him. Naturally, the conversation dealt with the trail and its dangers.

"You would hardly think," said the Cuban, "that, a hundred years ago, a stone-built road, as straight as an arrow, ran from Cap Haitien to Millot, and that over it, Toussaint l'Ouverture, 'the Black Napoleon,' was wont to ride at breakneck speed, and Christophe, 'the black Emperor,' drove his gaudy carriage with much pomp and display."

To those who take the road from Cap Haitien to Millot today, the existence of that ancient highway seems incredible. Yet, though only a century old, it is almost as hopelessly lost as the road in the Sahara Desert over which, once, toiling slaves in Egypt dragged the huge stones of which the Pyramids of Ghizeh were built.

Stuart and the Cuban had made a late start. In spite of the powerful political influence which the Cuban seemed to wield, his departure had been fraught with suspicion. The Military Governor, a gigantic coal-black negro, had at first refused to grant permission for Polliovo to visit the Citadel; the Commandant of Marines had given him a warning which was almost an ultimatum.

Manuel, with great suavity, had overset the former and defied the latter. His story was of the smoothest. He was a military strategist, he declared, and General Leborge had asked him to investigate the citadel, in order to determine its value as the site for a modern fort.

Stuart's part in the adventure was outwardly simple. No one thought it worth while to question him, and he accompanied the Cuban as a guide and horse-boy.

Although the road improved as the higher land was reached, it was dusk when the two riders arrived at the foothills around Millot.

Dark fell quickly, and, with the dark, came a low palpitating rumble, that distant throbbing of sound, that malevolent vibrance which gives to every Haitian moonlit night an oppression and a fear all its own.

"Rhoo-oo-oom—Rhoo-oo-oom—Rhoo-oo-oom!"

Muffled, dull, pulsating, unceasing, the thrummed tom-tom set all the air in motion. The vibrance scarcely seemed to be sound, rather did it seem to be a slower tapping of air-waves on the drum of the ear, too low to be actually heard, but yet beating with a maddening persistence.

There was a savagery in the sound, so disquieting, that a deep sigh of relief escaped from the boy's lungs when he saw the lights of Millot twinkling in the distance. Somehow, the presence of houses and people took away the sinister sound of the tom-tom and made it seem like an ordinary drum.

Millot, in the faint moonlight, revealed itself as a small village, nestling under high mountains. Signs of former greatness were visible in the old gates which flanked the opening into its main street, but the greater part of the houses were thatched huts.

When at the very entrance of the village, there came a ringing challenge,

"Halt! Who goes there?"

"A visitor to the General," was Manuel's answer.

The barefoot sentry, whose uniform consisted of a forage cap, a coat with one sleeve torn off and a pair of frayed trousers, but whose rifle was of the most up-to-date pattern, was at once joined by several others, not more splendidly arrayed than himself.

As with one voice, they declared that the general could not be disturbed, but the Cuban carried matters with a high hand. Dismounting, he ordered one of the sentries to precede him and announce his coming, and bade Stuart see that the horses were well looked after and ready for travel in the morning, "or his back should have a taste of the whip."

This phrase, while it only increased the enmity the soldiers felt toward the "white," had the effect of removing all suspicion from Stuart, which, as the lad guessed, was the reason for Manuel's threat. Feeling sure that the boy would have the same animosity to his master that they felt, the soldiers seized the opportunity to while away the monotonous hours of their duty in talk.

"What does he want, this 'white'?" they asked, suspiciously.

"Like all whites," answered Stuart, striving to talk in the character of the negro horse-boy, "he wants something he has no right to have."

"And what is that?"

"Information. He says he is a military strategist, and is going to make La Ferrière, up there, a modern fort."

"He will never get there," said one of the soldiers.

"You think not?"

"It is sure that he will not get there. Permission is refused always, Yes. The General is afraid lest a 'white' should find the buried money."

"Christophe's treasure?" queried the boy, innocently. He had never heard of this treasure before, but rightly guessed that if it were supposed to be hidden in the Citadel of the Black Emperor, it must have been placed there by no one but the grim old tyrant himself.

"But surely. Yes. You, in the south"—Stuart had volunteered the information that he came from the southern part of the island—"have you not heard the story of Dimanche (Sunday) Esnan?"

"I never heard it, No," Stuart answered.

"It was of strange, Yes," the soldier proceeded. "Christophe was rich, ah, how rich! He had all the money of the republic. He spent it like an emperor. You shall see for yourself, if you look, what Christophe spent in building palaces, but no one shall say how much he spent on his own pleasures. He had a court, like the great courts of Europe, and not a 'white' in them. Ah, he was very rich and powerful, Christophe. It is said that, when he died, he left 65,000,000 gourdes (then worth about $15,000,000) and this he buried, should he need money in order to escape. But, as even an ignorant like you will know, he did not escape."

"I know," replied Stuart, "he blew out his brains."

"Right over there, he did it!" the soldier agreed, pointing into the night. "But listen to the story of the treasure:

"When I was but a little older than a boy like you, into the Vache d'Or (a former gambling-house of some fame) there strolled this Dimanche Esnan. He swaggered in, as one with plenty of money in his pocket.

"Upon the table he threw some coins.

"The croupier stared down at those coins, with eyes as cold and fixed as those of a fer-de-lance ready to strike. The play at the table stopped.

"It was a moment!

"The coins were Spanish doubloons!"

"A pirate hoard?" suggested Stuart.

"It was thought. But this Dimanche had not been off the island for years! And the buccaneers' treasure is at Tortugas, as is well known.

"This Dimanche was at once asked if he had found Christophe's treasure, for where else would a man find Spanish doubloons of a century ago? It was plain, Yes!

"Well, what would you? President Hippolyte sent for him. He offered to make him a general, a full general, if he would but tell where he had found the treasure. He showed him the uniform. It was gold laced, yes, gold lace all over! Dimanche was nearly tempted, but not quite.

"Then they let him come back here, to Cap Haitien, Yes. All the day and all the night he was kept under watch. Ah, that was a strict watch! Every one of the guards thought that he might be the one to get clue to the place of the buried treasure, look you!

"But the general here, at that time, was not a patient man, No! Besides, he wanted the treasure. He wanted it without having the President of the Republic know. With sixty-five million gourdes he might push away the President and be president himself, who knows?

"What would you? The general put Dimanche in prison and put him to the question (torture) but Dimanche said nothing. Ah, he was stubborn, that Dimanche. He said nothing, nothing! The general did not dare to kill him, for he knew that the President had given orders to have the man watched.

"So the prison doors were set open. Pouf! Away disappears Dimanche and has not been seen since. He still carries the secret of the treasure of Christophe—that is, if he is not dead."

"But didn't the President try to find the hoard on his own account?" asked Stuart.

"But, most surely! My father was one of the soldiers in the party which searched in all the wonderful palaces that Christophe had built for himself in 'Without Worry,' in 'Queen's Delight,' in 'The Glory,' in 'Beautiful View,' yes, even in the haunted Citadel of La Ferrière. No, I should not have liked to do that, it is surely haunted. But they found nothing.

"Me, I think that the money is in the citadel. Has not the ghost of Christophe been seen to walk there? And why should the ghost walk if it had not a reason to walk? Eh?"

"That does seem reasonable," answered Stuart, in response to the soldier's triumphant tone.

"But, most sure! So, Boy," the guard concluded, "it is easy to see why the General does not like any 'white' to go to the Citadel. Perhaps the 'white,' whose horses you look after, has seen Dimanche. Who knows? So he will not be let get up there. You may be sure of that."

"One can't ever say," answered the boy. "I must be ready for the morning," and, with a word of farewell, he sauntered into the village of Millot, to find some kind of stabling and food for the horses, and, if possible, some shelter for himself.

Morning found Stuart outside the door of the general's "mansion," a straw-thatched building, comprising three rooms and a narrow brick-paved verandah. From what the soldiers had said the night before, the boy had not the slightest expectation of the Cuban's success.

He had not waited long, however, before Manuel came out through the door, obsequiously followed by a coal-black general daubed with gold lace—most of which was unsewn and hanging in tatters, and all of which was tarnished. He was strongly, even violently, urging upon Manuel the need of an escort. The Cuban not only disdained the question, but, most evidently, disdained and disregarded the man.

This extraordinary scene was closed by the General, the commandant of the entire commune, holding out his hand for a tip. Manuel put a five-gourdes bill (two dollars and a half) into the outstretched palm, and mounted his horse to an accompaniment of a profusion of thanks.

A short distance out of Millot, the two riders came to the ruins of Christophe's palace of "Without Worry" (Sans Souci). It was once a veritable palace, situated on the top of a small hill overlooking a deep ravine. Great flights of stone steps led up to it, while terrace upon terrace of what once were exquisitely kept gardens, filled with the finest statuary, stepped to the depths below.

Now, the gardens are waste, the statuary broken and the terraces are washed into gullies by the rains. The palace itself is not less lamentable. The walls are crumbling. Everything movable from the interior has been looted. Trees grow outward from the upper windows, and, in the cracks of masonry and marble floors, a tropic vegetation has sprung up. Moss covers the mosaics, and the carved woodwork has become the prey of the worm.

A little further on, at a hut which the General had described, Manuel and Stuart left their horses, and then began the steep climb up La Ferrière. From the steaming heat of the plain below, the climbers passed into the region of cold. The remains of a road were there, but the track was so indistinct as to render it difficult to follow.

"Where the dense forest begins," Manuel explained, "we shall find a warder. I would rather be without him, but the General does not dare to send a message that a 'white' may visit the Citadel unaccompanied. Besides, I doubt if we could find the way, though once this was a wide road, fit for carriage travel, on which the Black Emperor drove in pomp and state to his citadel. It is incredible!"

"What is incredible?" asked Stuart.

"That Christophe should have been able to make these negroes work for him as no people in the world have worked since the days when the Pharaohs of Egypt built the Pyramids. You will see the vast size of the Citadel. You see the steepness of the mountain. Consider it!

"The materials for the whole huge pile of building and the three hundred cannon with which it was fortified, were dragged up these steep mountain scarps and cliffsides by human hands. Christophe employed the troops mercilessly in this labor and subdued mutiny by the simple policy of not only shooting the mutineers, but also a corresponding number of innocent men, as well, just to teach a lesson. Whole villages were commandeered. Sex made no difference. Women worked side by side with men, were whipped side by side with men, and, if they weakened, were knifed or shot and thrown into a ditch. One of Christophe's overseers is said to have boasted that he could have made a roadway of human bones from Sans Souci to the summit."

The words "bloody ruffian" were on Stuart's lips, but, just in time, he remembered his character, and replied instead,

"But Christophe was a great man!"

The boy knew well that though Toussaint L'Ouverture, the "Black Napoleon," had truly been a great man in every sense of the word, a liberator, general and administrator, the Haitians think little of him, because he believed that blacks, mulattoes and whites should have an equal chance. Dessalines and Christophe, monsters of brutality, are the heroes of Haiti, because they massacred everyone who was not coal-black.

Manuel cast a sidelong glance at Stuart, smiling inwardly at the boy's attempt to maintain his disguise, that disguise which the Cuban had so quickly pierced, and shrugged his shoulders.

"What would you!" he rejoined. "You see yourself, it is the only government that Haitians understand. To this day, a century later, this part of the island is better than the south, because of the impress of the reign of Christophe. Nothing changes Haiti!"

"The Americans?" queried Stuart, trying to put a note of dislike into his voice, but intensely interested in his own question.

"They have changed nothing!" declared the Cuban, emphatically. "They have painted the faces of the coast towns, and that is all. You heard that drum, the night before last? Not until the tom-tom has ceased to beat in Haiti, can anything be changed."

He rose, threw away the stump of his cigar, and motioned to the boy to take up the trail.

A few hundred yards higher, a raucous shout halted them.

There was a rustle of branches, and a negro colossus, of the low-browed, heavy-jawed type, plunged through the thicket and barred the path.

Bareheaded, barefooted, his shirt consisting of a piece of cloth with holes for head and arms, his trousers torn to tatters by thorns, the warder of the Citadel looked what he was, a Caco machete man, little removed from the ferocity of African savagery.

To his shout, the Cuban deigned no answer.

He broke a switch from a bush, walked toward the negro guard with a contemptuous look and lashed him across the face with the switch, ordering him to lead the way.

Stuart expected to see the Cuban cut down with one stroke of the machete.

Far from it. Cowed at once, the negro cringed, as to a master, and, without a word as to Manuel's authority, led the way up the trail.

A hundred yards higher, all sign of a path was lost. The negro warder was compelled to use his machete to cut a way through thorny underbrush and creepers in order to make a path for the "white's" feet.

The afternoon was well advanced when openings amid the trees showed, beetling overhead, the gray walls of the Citadel. An hour's further climbing brought them to the guard-house, where eight men watch continually, each relief for a period of a month, against the intrusion of strangers into Christophe's Citadel.

An irregularly disposed clump of posts, stuck into the ground, supported a rusted and broken tin roof, without walls, but boasting a brushwood pile on one side—such was the entire barracks of the La Ferrière garrison. The furniture consisted only of a log on which to sit, a few cooking utensils, and a pile of rags in the driest corner.

True, there was plenty of room in the Citadel. Many a chamber in the ruined place was dry and sheltered from the weather, many a corner was there where the watchers could have made themselves warm and comfortable. They were not forbidden to sleep there. On the contrary, they were encouraged. But never a one would do so. They declared the place haunted and were in a state of terror even to be near it.

Manuel, after pausing for a moment to take his breath, strode up to the group.

"Get in there, some of you!" he ordered, "And show me the way. I want to see over the place."

A chorus of wails arose. The guards shrank and cowered at the suggestion. Their terror was more than panicky, it was even hysterical. They shook with convulsive jerks of fear, as though they had a spasm disease.

"Christophe!" cried one of them, in a sort of howl. "Christophe! For three days he is here, Yes! We see him walk, Yes! If we go in, he will make us jump off the cliff!"

And another added, with an undertone of superstitious horror,

"And his ghost will be waiting at the bottom to carry our ghosts away!"

"Fools!" declared Manuel, "open the door!"

He pointed to where the huge, rusty iron-bound door frowned in the blank wall of gray stone.

The negro guards hung back and gabbled together, but Manuel turned upon them fiercely with uplifted switch. At that, the giant warder, who had already acknowledged the mastership, slouched forward and pulled open the creaking door, leaving a dark opening from which came the smell of foul air and poisonous vegetation.

Manuel motioned with his head for Stuart to precede him.

The boy hesitated. He was brave enough, but the terror of the negroes was catching. He would not have admitted to being afraid, but there was a lump in his throat and his legs felt unsteady.

The Cuban, who felt sure that Stuart was not the negro horse-boy that he seemed, judged this appearance of fear as evidence that the boy was still playing a part, and turned on him with a snarl.

"Get in there, you!"

Screwing up his courage, Stuart stepped forward, though hesitatingly and unwillingly. Just as he crossed the threshold, the giant warder reached out a gaunt hand and pulled him back.

"Not that way!" he said. "Two steps more, Boy, and you are dead!"

Manuel started. From his pocket he took a portable electric light and flashed it upon the ground just within the entrance.

The negro guard was right. Immediately before him lay a deep pit, how deep there was no means of saying. Once it had been covered with a trap-door, which could be worked from the Inner Citadel. Thus Christophe, if he pleased, could send a message of welcome to his visitors, and drop them to a living death with the words of hospitality on his lips.

"If I had gone first," said Manuel quietly, turning to the guards, "not one of you would have said a word!"

The negroes slunk away under his gaze. The accusation was true. They had no love for the "whites." Only the fact that they believed Stuart to be a negro boy had saved him.

The boy looked down at that profound dungeon, from which rose a faint stench, and shuddered.

There was a heavy pause. Manuel was debating whether he dare try and force the guards to show the way. If he ordered it, he would have to force it through, or the prestige he had won would be lost. He dared not. As between the terror of a white man's gun, and the terror of a "ha'nt," the latter was the more powerful.

Motioning Stuart to enter and showing the narrow ledge around the pit with the spotlight, he followed. Then he turned to the guards clustered outside.

"Close the door!" he ordered, curtly.

This command was obeyed with alacrity. The negro guards were only too anxious to see that hole in the wall shut. Suppose the ghost of Christophe should come gliding out among them!

So far, the Cuban was safe. He had reached the Citadel and entered it. He had no fear that the warders would open it again to spy on him. Their terror was too real.

Raising the spot-light so that it flashed full upon Stuart's face, the Cuban spoke.

"Understand me, now," he said curtly, and with a hard ring in his voice. "How much of your story may be true and how much false I have not yet found out. But, if what you say about hating Leborge is true, I will put you in a place where you will be able to see him. You have a pistol, I know. If you see Leborge raise pistol or knife against me, shoot, and shoot quickly! I will make you rich!"

Stuart thought to himself that if the conspirators were to come to quarreling, that was the very time he would keep still. He, certainly, had no desire for bloodshed, nor any intention to fire at anybody, if he could help it. But he only answered,

"I understand."

Manuel's intention was no less concealed. He planned either to reveal the boy to his fellow-conspirators, or else, to reveal him to the negro warders as a white intruder. Either way, he figured, there would be an end to the boy.

By the light of his lamp, consulting a small manuscript chart of the ruin, Manuel passed through many tortuous passages and dark chambers until he came to a ruined wall. Climbing a few feet up the crumbling stones, he set his eye to a crevice, nodded as though satisfied, wrenched away several more stones, laying these down silently and beckoned Stuart to come beside him.

The boy looked down on a circular hall, the outer arc of which was pierced with ruined windows opening to the sky.

"Leborge will sit there!" whispered Manuel, pointing. "Kill him, and you will be rich!"

Stuart nodded. He did not trust himself to speak.

Walking as silently as he could, Manuel left the place, pondering in his own mind what he was going to do with the boy. Should he reveal the secret and have his fellow-conspirators kill him? Should he turn him over to the machetes of the negroes? Or should he kill the boy, himself? One thing he had determined—that Stuart should not reach the plains below, alive.

And Stuart, in that hole of the ruined wall, crouched and watched. Of what was to happen in that room below, what dark plot he was to hear, he had no knowledge. Yet, over his eager desire to find out this conspiracy against the United States, above his anxiety with regard to the fate of his father, one question loomed in ever larger and blacker proportions—

He had got into the Citadel. How was he to get out?

The Ghost of Christophe

Manuel was no coward. Somewhere, back in his Spanish ancestry, had been a single drop of an Irish strain, adding a certain combativeness to the gallantry of his race. That drop, too, mixed badly with Spanish treachery, and made him doubly dangerous.

Certainly the Cuban was no coward. But, as he came out from the murk of those chambers with their rotting floors, many of them undermined by oubliettes and dungeons, he felt a chill of fear. Even the occasional bursts of sunshine through the cloud-fog which perpetually sweeps over La Ferrière did not hearten him. He passed into the open space back of the outer walls and set himself to climb the long flight of stone steps that led to the battlements, where, he thought, his fellow conspirators might be. But, on the summit, he found himself alone.

The battlements cowed his spirits. With walls fifteen feet thick, wide enough to allow a carriage to be driven upon them, they looked over a sheer drop of two thousand feet. Sinister and forbidding, even the sunlight could not lessen their grimness.

As if in memory of the hundreds of victims who had been bidden jump off those ramparts, merely for Christophe's amusement, or who had been hurled, screaming, as penalty for his displeasure, a ruddy moss feeding upon decay, has spread over the stones, and this moss, ever kept damp by the cloud-banks which wreathe the Citadel continually is moistly red, like newly shed blood. In cracks and corners, fungi of poisonous hues adds another touch of wickedness. Manuel shivered with repulsion. Probably not in all the world, certainly not in the Western Hemisphere, is there a ruin of such historic terror as the Citadel of the Black Emperor on the summit of La Ferrière.[1]

[1] This ruin, now, is nominally in territory under the jurisdiction of an American provost-marshal. It is therefore less difficult of access than formerly, but it is still considered unsafe for travelers.

A gleam of sun revealed the extraordinary impregnability of the place. The double-walled entrance from the hillside, pierced by but a single gate, could only be battered down by heavy artillery, and no guns powerful enough for such a feat could be brought up the hill. The Inner Citadel, access to which was only by a long flight of steps, is unapproachable from any other point, and a handful of defenders could keep an army at bay.

The cliff-side is as sheer as Gibraltar, affording not even a foothold for the most venturesome climber. The walls are built upon its very verge and are as solid as the rock itself. Its gray mass conveys a sense of enormous power. "It towers upon the last and highest precipice," says Hesketh Prichard, "like some sinister monster of the elder world, ready to launch itself forth upon the spreading lands below."

The Citadel commands the whole of the Plain of the North clear to the distant sea. At its south-eastern end it faces toward the frontier of St. Domingo, the sister republic, fifty miles away. Christophe built it as a central base, controlling the only roads and passes which command the range from Dondon to Vallière, and rendering attack impossible, from the southern side, through Marmalade. (Many names in Haiti give an irresistible appearance of being comic, such as the Duke of Lemonade, Duke of Marmalade, Baron the Prophet Daniel, and Colonel the Baron Roast Beef, but they are intended seriously.)

Manuel had gazed over the landscape but a few moments when the sun was veiled in one of the cold, raw cloud-fogs which continually sweep the summit. Billowing, dank masses hurtled about him, blotting out even the outlines of the ruin. For several minutes the grey mists enwreathed him, then, as they lightened, the Cuban saw before him, shadow-like and strange, the figure of the Black Emperor himself.

The warders' terror of the ghost of Christophe cramped Manuel's heart for a moment and he fell back. His hand flashed to his pocket, none the less.

The figure laughed, a harsh coarse laugh which Manuel knew and recognized at once.

"General Leborge," he exclaimed, surprise and self-annoyance struggling in his voice. "It is you!"

"But Yes, my friend, it is I. You see, I am not so daring as you. I came secretly. I have been here three days, waiting for you."

"But the meeting was set for today!"

"It is true. But it was more difficult for me to get here than for you. See you, as a stranger you had not the suspicion of intrusion to combat. No, if it were known that I were here, there would be political difficulties—ah, many! Yes!"

The Cuban nodded. He was not especially interested in the political embroilments of his co-conspirator. As a matter of fact, the plot accomplished, it was Manuel's purpose to let enough of the truth leak out to make it seem that Leborge had been a traitor to the Haitian Republic.

"Have you seen Cecil?" he asked.

"Not yet, No!" answered the negro general. "Me, I had thought he would come with you."

"He didn't. And he wasn't on the road from Cap Haitien, either. Queer, too. First time I ever knew him to fail."

"So! But I have a feeling he will not fail. He will be here today. Come down to the place of meeting. I have some food and we can have a mouthful while waiting for him."

The big negro cast a look at himself.

"I do not think we shall be interrupted, No!" he commented.

The Cuban showed his teeth in the gleam of a quick smile.

"The guards are too much afraid of the ghost of Christophe to dare enter the place," he said. "That was a good idea of yours."

The two men turned away from the battlements to the steps which led down toward the dwelling rooms, and Manuel laid finger on lip.

"It is well to be a ghost," he said, "but if the guards should chance to hear me talking to the ghost, they might begin to think. And thinking, my dear Leborge, is sometimes dangerous."

The huge negro nodded assent and hung back while Manuel descended the stair.

At the entrance into the high room, ringed with windows, in a small ruined opening of which Stuart crouched watching, Manuel waited for Leborge. Together they entered.

At the door of the room the negro started back with an exclamation of astonishment, and even Manuel paused.

On a square block of stone in the center of the room, which Manuel could have sworn was not there when he looked into the chamber a short half-hour before, sat Guy Cecil, complacently puffing at a briar pipe. His tweeds were as immaculate as though he had just stepped from the hands of his valet, and his tan shoes showed mark neither of mud nor rough trails. Manuel's quick glance caught these details and they set him wondering.

"By the Ten Finger-Bones!" ejaculated Leborge. "How did you get in here?"

"Why?" asked Cecil, in mild surprise.

"Polliovo didn't see you come. I didn't see you come."

"No?"

The negation was insolent in its carelessness.

"But how did you get in?"

The Englishman took his pipe from his mouth, and, with the stem, pointed negligently to a window.

"That way," he said.

The negro blustered out an oath, but was evidently impressed, and looked at his fellow-conspirator with superstitious fear.

The Cuban, more curious and more skeptical, went straight to the window and looked out. The crumbling mortar-dust on the sill had evidently been disturbed, seeming to make good the Englishman's story, but, from the window, was a clear drop of four hundred feet of naked rock, without even a crack to afford a finger-hold, while the precipitous descent fell another fifteen hundred feet. To climb was a feat manifestly impossible.

"Permit me to congratulate you on your discovery of wings, Senor Cecil," remarked Manuel, with irony.

The Englishman bowed, as at a matter-of-course compliment, and, by tacit agreement, the subject dropped.

Yet Manuel's irritation was hard to hide. Not the least of the reasons for his animosity to Cecil was the Englishman's undoubted ability to cover his movements. In the famous case when the two conspirators had negotiated an indigo concession in San Domingo and the profits had suddenly slipped through Manuel's fingers, the Cuban was sure that the Englishman had made a winning, but he had no proof. Likewise, with this plot in hand, Manuel feared lest he should be outmanoeuvred at the last.

Following Cecil's example, Leborge and Manuel rolled out to the center of the room some blocks that had fallen from the walls, and sat down. Stuart noticed that the Cuban so placed himself that he was well out of a possible line of fire between the negro general and the embrasure where the boy was hidden. This carefulness, despite its air of negligence, reminded Stuart of the rôle he was expected to play, and he concentrated his attention on the three conspirators.

Although the Cuban was apparently the only one who had reason to suspect being overheard, the three men talked in low tones. The language used was French, as Stuart gleaned from a word or two which reached his ears, but the subject of the conversation escaped him. One phrase, however, attracted his attention because it was so often repeated, and Stuart surmised that this phrase must bear an important relation to the main subject of the meeting. The boy did not fail to realize that a conference so important that it could only be held in so secret a place must be of extraordinary gravity. This phrase was——

FOR A HUNDRED FEET THEY FELL AND STUART CLOSED HIS
EYES IN SICKENING DIZZINESS FOR A HUNDRED FEET THEY FELL
AND STUART CLOSED HIS EYES IN SICKENING DIZZINESS

"Mole St. Nicholas."

The words held no meaning for Stuart, though he had seen reference to
them in his father's papers. He suspected that the phrase might be some
catch-word referring to a subject too dangerous for mention, possibly the
Presidency of Haiti. Following out this theme, the boy guessed that he was
a witness to the hatching of one of the political revolutions, which, from
time to time, have convulsed the Republic of Haiti. If so, the matter was
serious, for, as the boy knew, ever since the treaty of 1915, the United
States was actively interested in forcing the self-determination of Haiti,
meanwhile holding the country under a virtual protectorate. Such a
revolution, therefore, would be a deliberate attack upon the United States.

This impression was heightened by his catching the words "naval base,"
which could only deal with possible developments in a state of war. Stuart
strained his ears to the utmost, but isolated words were all that he could
glean.

Later, Stuart was to learn that his guess was at fault in general, but that
the conclusion he had reached—namely, that injury to the United States
was intended—was not far wide of the mark.

As the conference proceeded, it became evident to the hidden observer
that the relations between the conspirators were growing strained. The
Cuban seemed to be in taunting mood. The veins on the negro general's
bull neck began to swell, and he turned and called Manuel,

"Pale Toad!"

A moment after, his raucous voice insulted the Englishman with the
description,

"Snake that does not even hiss!"

Stuart expected to see violence follow these words, but the Cuban only
moved restlessly under the insult; the Englishman smiled. It was a pleasant
smile, but Stuart was keen enough to grasp that a man who smiles when he
is insulted must either be a craven or a dangerous man with an inordinate
gift of self-control. Cecil could not be a coward, or such men as Manuel
and Leborge would not so evidently fear him, therefore the other character
must befit him.

Another word which repeated itself frequently was——

"Panama."

This confirmed Stuart in his suspicions that the conspiracy, whatever it might portend, was directed against the authority of the United States, since the Panama Canal Zone is under American jurisdiction.

The conference was evidently coming to a crisis. The negro was becoming excited, the Cuban nervous, the Englishman more immovable than ever.

Came a sudden movement, following upon some phrase uttered by Manuel, but unheard by the boy, and the Cuban and Leborge leaped to their feet, a revolver in each man's right hand.

Spoke the Englishman, in a quiet voice, but sufficiently deepened by excitement to reach the boy's ears:

"Is there any reason, Gentlemen, why I should not shoot both of you and finish this little affair myself?"

A revolver glittered in his hand, though no one had seen the action of drawing.

In the flash of a second, Stuart understood Manuel's plot. It was the Cuban who had provoked the negro to draw his weapon, counting on the boy's shooting his supposed enemy, as had been agreed upon. Then Manuel would drag him out of his hiding-place and kill him for an eavesdropper. He crouched, motionless, and watched.

"Sit down, and put up your weapons," continued Cecil, his voice still tense enough to be heard clearly. "This is childishness. Our plans need all three of us. It will be time enough to quarrel when we come to divide the spoils. First, the spoils must be won."

Negro and Cuban, without taking their eyes from other, each fearing that the other might take an advantage, realized from Cecil's manner, that he must have the drop on them. With a simultaneous movement, they put away their guns. The negro sat down, beaten. Manuel, with a swift and hardly noticeable side-step, moved a little nearer to Cecil, putting himself almost within knife-thrust distance.

A slight, a very slight elevation of the barrel of the tiny revolver glittering in the Englishman's hand warned the Cuban that the weapon was covering his heart. An even slighter narrowing of the eyelids warned him that Cecil was fully ready to shoot.

With a low curse, the Cuban retreated to his stone and sat down. He did not sprawl loosely in dejection, as had the negro, but he sat with one foot beside the stone and his body leaning half-forward, his muscles tense, like a forest cat awaiting its spring.

The conference came to a head quickly, as Stuart saw. The outbreak of mistrust and hostility, followed by discussion, proved how closely linked were the plotters. Yet each man wanted the business done as quickly as possible, and wanted to be free from the danger of assassination by his comrades.

Leborge drew from his pocket a paper which he showed to the other two, and, in turn, Manuel and Cecil produced documents, the Englishman using his left hand only and never dropping the barrel of his revolver. Few words were exchanged, and these in the low tones in which the conference had been carried on before. Of the contents of the papers, Stuart could not even guess. Whatever they were, they seemed to be satisfactory, for, so far as the boy could judge, harmony returned among the conspirators. But the Englishman kept wary watch with his gun.

"All goes well, then," concluded Leborge, rising and shivering in the damp air, for the clouds were eddying through the ruined windows in raw and gusty blasts.

"It can be done next spring!" declared the Cuban.

"It will be done, as agreed," was the Englishman's more cautious statement.

"Then," said Manuel, raising his voice a trifle in a way which Stuart knew he was meant to hear, "the sooner I get down to Cap Haitien the better. I had trouble enough to get up."

"It might be well," suggested the Englishman, "if Leborge should repeat his trick of appearing as the ghost of Christophe. The guards will be so frightened that they will think of nothing else, and you will be able to get away without any unpleasantness."

"And you?" queried the Cuban. "How will you go?"

Again the Englishman nodded toward the window.

"I will use the wings you were kind enough to say I must possess," he answered, enigmatically.

Peering out cautiously from his post of observation in the embrasure, Stuart saw that both Manuel and Leborge hesitated at the entrance to the dark passage which led from the Dining Hall and Queen's Chamber to the inner court, from whence went the paths leading respectively to the outer gate, whither Manuel must go, and to the battlements, where Leborge was to reappear as the ghost of Christophe.

"You are afraid of each other?" queried Cecil, with his faint smile. "Well, perhaps you have reason! I will go through the passage with both of you. As I said before, each of us needs the other."

Relief and hate passed like shadows across the faces of Leborge and Manuel. Each had intended to kill the other in the dark of those passages, each had feared that he might be slain himself. As Cecil knew, once out in the open, mutual distrust and watchfulness would ensure the keeping of the peace.

Stuart, listening intently for the sound of shots, heard in the distance the Englishman's voice:

"I forgot my pipe. I'll just go back for it."

And then he heard steps coming at a light, but fast run. Evidently Cecil wanted to gain time.

The Englishman came in swiftly, picked up his pipe—which he had left on the stone—slipped across toward the window, moved a loosened stone and drew out from a cavity in the wall a green bundle from which some straps were hanging. These he buckled on as a body-harness. Stuart had never seen fingers that moved so quickly, or which had less appearance of hurry.

A thought struck him. Impulsively, he leaped from the embrasure.

A glitter told him that the gun was covering him.

He spoke breathlessly.

"Manuel expected me to kill Leborge. He'll kill me for not doing it."

In answer to a commanding look of interrogation, Stuart went on:

"I'm an American, and straight. I'll tell you all about it, later. Guess there isn't much time, now. Take me with you."

Cecil knew men. He looked at the boy, piercingly, and answered:

"Very well. If you've got the nerve."

"I have!"

Eye flashed to eye.

Came the decision:

"Your belt's too small. Take mine!"

The Englishman unfastened his own belt, grasped the boy by the shoulders, spun him round, ran the belt under his arms and through the two sides of the harness he had strapped on himself. He took a step and a heave and both were on the window-sill.

At the sight of the abyss below, a sudden panic caught Stuart's breath and heart, and he seemed to choke.

"What do we do?" he gasped.

"We jump!" said Cecil.

They leaped clear.

For a hundred feet they fell, and Stuart closed his eyes in that sickening dizziness which comes from a high fall.

Then he felt Cecil's arm grip him in a bear hug, and, a second after, his breast bone seemed to cave in, as a sudden jerk and strain came on the strap by which he was bound to the Englishman.

Instinctively he tried to squirm free, but the grip and the strap held firm.

Then the falling motion changed into a slow rocking see-saw, coupled with a sense of extraordinary lightness, and Stuart, looking overhead, saw the outstretched circle of a modern parachute.

The Isle of the Buccaneers

Swaying in sea-sick fashion, Stuart saw the forests, far below, seem to rise up to meet him. Under the influence of the double motion of drop and roll, the whole earth seemed to be rocking, and the sense of the void beneath him made Stuart feel giddy and faint. The fall was slower than he had expected.

Soon, a damp heat, rising from below, warned the boy that they were approaching the ground, and, a second or two later, the Englishman said quietly:

"We are going to hit the trees. Cover your face and head with your arms. You won't be hurt, but there is no sense in having one's eyes scratched out."

In fact, the trees were very near. Stuart cast one look down, and then, following the advice given, covered his face. A quarter of a minute later, his legs and the lower half of his body plunged into twigs and foliage. The parachute, released from a part of the weight which had held it steady, careened, was caught by a sidewise gust of wind, and, bellying out like a sail, it dragged the two aerial travelers through the topmost branches in short, vicious jerks which made Stuart feel as though he were being pulled apart. This lasted but a minute or two, however, when the parachute itself, torn, and caught in the branches, came to anchor.

"I fancy we had better climb down," remarked Cecil, cheerfully, and, at the same time, Stuart realized that the belt, which had grappled him tight to the Englishman's harness, had been loosened.

The boy drew a long breath, for his lungs had been tightly compressed during the downward journey, and, instinctively, reached out for a branch sufficiently strong to support him.

The Englishman, a man of quicker action, had already swung clear and was descending the tree with a lithe agility that seemed quite out of keeping with his quiet and self-possessed manner. The boy, despite his youth, came down more clumsily. On reaching ground, he found his companion sedately polishing his tan boots with a tiny bit of rag he had taken from a box not much bigger than a twenty-five cent piece. Stuart's clothes were torn in half-a-dozen places, Cecil's tweeds were absolutely unharmed.

The Englishman caught the boy's thought and answered it.

"Explorers' Cloth," he said. "I have it made specially for me; you can hardly cut it with a knife."

Inwardly the boy felt that he ought to be able to carry on the conversation in the same light vein, but his nerves were badly shaken. His companion glanced at him.

"A bit done up, eh?" He took a metal container from his pocket, in shape like a short lead pencil, and poured out two tiny pellets into his palm.

"If you are not afraid of poison," he remarked amicably, "swallow these. They will pick you up at once."

The thought of poison had flashed into Stuart's mind. After all, the Englishman was just as much one of the conspirators as Manuel or Leborge, and might be just as anxious for the death of an eavesdropper. At the same time, the boy realized that he was absolutely in the Englishman's power, and that if Cecil wanted to get rid of him, there, in that thick forest, he had ample opportunity. To refuse the pellets might be even more dangerous than to accept them. Besides, there was a certain atmosphere of directness in Cecil, conspirator though the boy knew him to be, which forbade belief in so low-grade a manner of action as the use of poison.

He held out his hand for the pellets and swallowed them without a word.

A slight inclination of the head showed the donor's acceptance of the fact that he was trusted.

"Now, my lad," he said. "I think you ought to tell me something about yourself, and what you were doing in the Citadel. You asked me to save you from Manuel, and I have done so. Perhaps I have been hasty. But, in honor bound, you must tell me what you know and what you heard."

Through Stuart's veins, the blood was beginning to course full and free. The pellets which Cecil had given him—whatever they were—removed his fatigue as though it had been a cloak. They loosened the boy's tongue, also, and freely he told the Englishman all his affairs save for his cause in pursuing Manuel, which he regarded as a personal matter. He mentioned the only words he had overheard, while watching in the ruined Citadel and explained that the taunting of Leborge by Manuel, during the conference, had been only a ruse to provoke trouble, the Cuban hoping that the boy would shoot.

"And what general impression did you get from the meeting?" Cecil queried.

The boy hesitated, fearing to enrage his questioner.

"Well," he blurted out, "if I must say it, I think that you're plotting a revolution in this country, putting Leborge up as president, letting Manuel run the country, driving the United States clean out of it, and giving you the chance to take all sorts of commercial concessions for yourself."

The Englishman nodded his head.

"For a guess," he declared, "your idea is not half bad. Evidently, you have plenty of imagination. The only trouble with your summing up of the situation, my boy, is that it is wrong in every particular. If you did not learn any more than that from the conference, your information is quite harmless. I suppose I can count on your never mentioning this meeting?"

Stuart thought for a moment.

"No," he said, "I can't promise that."

The Englishman lifted his eyebrows slightly.

"And why?"

Stuart found it difficult to say why. He had a feeling that to swear silence would, in a sense, make him a party to the conspiracy, whatever it might be.

"I—I've got it in for Manuel," he said lamely, though conscious, as he said it, that the reply would not satisfy.

Cecil looked at him through narrowed eyelids.

"I suppose you know that I would have no scruples in shooting you if you betrayed us," he remarked.

Stuart looked up.

"I don't know it," he answered. "Manuel or Leborge might do it, but I think you'd have a lot of scruples in shooting an unarmed boy."

"Surely you can't expect me to save your life merely to run my own neck in a noose?"

"That's as good as admitting that what you're doing might run your neck into a noose," commented Stuart shrewdly, if a little imprudently.

"All right. But you must play fair. I have helped you. In honor, you can't turn that help against me."

It was a definite deadlock. The boy realized that, while the Englishman was not likely to put a bullet through his head, as either Manuel or Leborge would have done, he was none the less likely to arrange affairs so that there would be no chance for talk. Haitian prisons were deathtraps. Also Cecil's declaration that an abuse of kindness would be dishonorable had a great deal of weight with the boy. His father had taught him the fine quality of straight dealing.

"Look here, sir," he said, after a pause. "You said that I hadn't got the right idea as to what you three were doing."

"You haven't."

"Then I can't betray it, that's sure! I'll promise, if you like, that, if I do ever find out the whole truth about this plot, and if it's something which, as an American, I oughtn't to let go by, I won't make any move in it until I know you've been warned in plenty of time. If it isn't, I'll say nothing. There's no reason why I should get Leborge or you in trouble. It's Manuel I'm after."

"If you'll promise that," said Cecil, "I fancy I can afford to let you go. I don't want you with me, anyway, for that Cuban dog would be sure that you had betrayed him to me, and he would suppose that I was going to betray him in turn. I'll land you in Cuba, and if you take my advice, you'll keep away from Haiti. It isn't healthy—for you."

Having thus settled Stuart's fate to his own satisfaction, Cecil climbed a little distance up the tree, caught the ropes of the parachute, and with much hauling, assisted by Stuart, he pulled the wreckage down and thrust it under a bush.

"The weather and the ants will make short work of that," he commented. "There won't be much of it left but the ribs in a week. And now, lad, we'll strike for the coast."

Though there seemed to Stuart no way of telling where they were, Cecil took a definite course through the jungle. They scrambled over and through the twisted tangle of undergrowth, creepers and lianas, and, in less than an hour, reached a small foot-path, bearing northwestward.

"I don't know this path," the Englishman remarked frankly, "but it's going in the direction I want, any way." A little later, he commented, "I fancy this leads to a village," and struck out into the jungle for a detour. On the further side of the village, he remarked, "I know where I am, now," and, thereafter, made no further comment upon the route. He talked very interestingly, however, about the insects, flowers and trees by the way, and, when dark came on, taught Stuart more about the stars than he had learned in all his years of schooling.

They walked steadily without a halt for food, even, from the late afternoon when the parachute had hit the trees, until about an hour after sunrise the next morning, when the faint trail that they had lately been following, suddenly came to an end on the bank of a narrow river, hardly more than a creek.

Putting a tiny flat instrument between his teeth, Cecil blew a shriek so shrill that it hurt Stuart's ears. It was repeated from a distance, almost immediately. Five minutes later the boy heard the "chug-chug" of a motor boat, and a small craft of racing pattern glided up to the bank.

"Got a passenger, Andy," he said to the sole occupant of the boat.

"Food for fishes?" came the grim query, in reply.

"Not yet; not this time, anyway. No, we'll just put him ashore at Cuba and see if he knows how to mind his own business."

The motor boat engineer grumbled under his breath. He was evidently not a man for half-measures. The blood of the old buccaneers ran in his veins. It was evident, though, that Cecil was master.

The two men aboard, Andy turned the head of the motor boat down the river and out to sea, shooting past the short water-front of the little village of Plaine du Nord at a bewildering speed. The Creoles had barely time to realize that there was something on the water before it was gone out of sight.

Despite its speed—which was in the neighborhood of thirty-two knots—the motor boat was built for sea use, and it ran along the coast of the Haitian north peninsula, past Le Borgne and St. Louis de Nord, like a scared dolphin. Arriving near Port-de-Paix, it hugged the shore of the famous lair of the buccaneers, Isle de Tortugas, and thence struck for the open sea.

"Tortugas!" commented Cecil, pointing to the rocky shores of the islet.

"That's where all the pirates came from, wasn't it?" queried Stuart, eager to break the silence of the journey.

"Pirates? No. The pirate haunts were more to the north. It was the stronghold of the buccaneers."

"I always thought pirates and buccaneers were the same thing," put in the boy.

"Far from it. Originally the buccaneers were hunters, and their name comes from boucan, a word meaning dried flesh. They hunted wild cattle and wild pigs on that island over there."

"Haiti?"

"It was called Hispaniola, then. The Spanish owned it, but had only a few settlements on the coast. The population was largely Carib, a savage race given to cannibalism. There seems little reason to doubt that even if the buccaneers did not actually smoke and cure human flesh, as the Caribs did, they traded in it and ate it themselves."

"Were the buccaneers Spaniards?" queried Stuart.

"No. French to begin with, and afterwards, many English joined them. That was just where the whole bloody business began. France protected the buccaneers, sent them aid and ammunition; even their famous guns—known as 'buccaneering pieces' and four and a half feet long—were all made in France. There was a steady demand for smoked meat and hides, and France was only too ready to get these from a Spanish colony without payment of any dues thereon.

"At the beginning of the seventeenth century the buccaneers—at that time only hunters—settled in small groups on the island of Hispaniola. Such a policy was dangerous. Time after time parties of Spanish soldiery raided the settlements, killing most of the hunters and putting the prisoners to the torture. In desperation, the buccaneers decided to abandon Hispaniola. They united their forces and sailed to the island of St. Kitts, nominally in the hands of Spain, but then inhabited only by Caribs.

"The French government at once extended its protection to St. Kitts, thus practically seizing it from Spain and claimed it as a possession. Great Britain agreed to support France in this illegal seizure and thus the little colony of St. Kitts was held safe under both French and English governments, which actually supported the hunting ventures of the buccaneers, and winked at the piratic raids which generally formed a part of the buccaneering expeditions.

"But it was not to be expected that the Spanish would keep still under the continual pillage of these plundering hunters. The Dons undertook to destroy the small vessels in which the buccaneers sailed and, before three years had passed, fully one-half of the buccaneers sailing from St. Kitts had been savagely slaughtered. These outrages prompted reprisals from the English and the French and thus the privateers came into the field."

"What's a privateer?" queried Stuart.

"I was just about to tell you," answered Cecil. "A privateer on the Caribbean and the Spanish Main, in those days, was a man who had sufficient money or sufficient reputation to secure a ship and a crew with which to wage war against the enemies of his country. As his own government had given nothing but permission to his venture, it gained nothing but glory from it. The privateer had the right to all the booty and plunder he could secure by capturing an enemy's ship, or raiding an enemy's settlement. The plunder was divided among the crew. Thus, a lucky voyage, in which, for example, a Spanish treasure-ship was captured, would make every member of the crew rich. Some of these privateers, after one or so prosperous voyages, settled down and became wealthy planters. The great Sir Francis Drake, on several of his voyages, went as a privateer."

"And I suppose the governments gained, by having a fleet of vessels doing their fighting, for which they needn't pay," commented the boy.

"Exactly. In a way, this was fair enough. The privateer took his chance, and, whether he won or lost, he was, at least, fighting for his country. But there were other men, unable to secure ships, and who could not obtain letters-of-marque from their governments, to whom loot and plunder seemed an easy way of gaining riches. Some of these were men from the crews of privateers that had disbanded, some were buccaneers. They claimed the same rights as privateers but differed in this—that they would attack any ship or settlement and plunder it at will. At first they confined themselves to small Spanish settlements only, but, later, their desires increased, and neutral ships and inoffensive villages were attacked.

"In order to put a stop to the raids of the buccaneering hunters, the Spaniards planned an organized destruction of all the wild cattle on Hispaniola, hoping thus to drive the ravagers away. It was a false move. The result of it was to turn the buccaneers into sea-rovers on an independent basis, ready for plunder and murder anywhere and everywhere. At this period they were called Filibusters, but, a little later, the word 'buccaneer' came to be used for the whole group of privateers, filibusters and hunters.

"The fury of both sides increased. So numerous and powerful did these sea-rovers become that all trade was cut off. Neutral vessels, even if in fleets, were endangered. With the cutting off of trade by sea, there was no longer any plunder for the rovers and from this cause came about the famous land expeditions, such as the sack of Maracaibo by Lolonnois the Cruel, and the historic capture of Panama by Morgan. Large cities were taken and held to ransom. Organized raids were made, accompanied by murder and rapine. The gallantry of privateering was degenerating into the bloody brutality of piracy.

"In 1632, a small group of French buccaneer hunters had left St. Kitts and, seeking a base nearer to Hispaniola, had attacked the little island of Tortugas, on which the Spanish had left a garrison of only twenty-five men. Every one of the Spaniards were killed. The buccaneers took possession, found the harbor to be excellent, and the soil of the island exceedingly fertile. As a buccaneer base, it was ideal. Filibusters saw the value of a base so close to Spanish holdings, realized the impregnability of the harbor and flocked thither. Privateers put in and brought their prizes. Tortugas began to prosper. In 1638 the Spaniards, taking advantage of a time when several large expeditions of buccaneers were absent, raided the place in force and shot, hanged, or tortured to death, every man, woman and child they captured. Only a few of the inhabitants escaped by hiding among the rocks. But the Spanish did not dare to leave a garrison.

"The buccaneers got together and under Willis, an Englishman, reoccupied the island. Although Willis was English, the greater part of the buccaneers with him were French and they gladly accepted a suggestion from the governor-general at St. Kitts to send a governor to Tortugas. In 1641 Governor Poincy succeeded in securing possession of the Isle of Tortugas for the Crown of France. Thus, having a shadow of protection thrown around it, and being afforded the widest latitude of conduct by its governor—who fully realized that it was nothing but a nest of pirates—Tortugas flamed into a mad prosperity.

"That little desert island yonder became the wildest and most abandoned place that the world probably has ever seen. Sea-rovers, slave-runners, filibusters, pirates, red-handed ruffians of every variety on land or sea made it their port of call. Everything could be bought there; everything sold. There was a market for all booty and every article—even captured white people for slaves—was exposed for sale. An adventurer could engage a crew of cut-throats at half-an-hour's notice. A plot to murder a thousand people in cold blood would be but street talk. Every crime which could be imagined by a depraved and gore-heated brain was of daily occurrence. It was a sink of iniquity.

"After France had taken possession of Tortugas, it came about quite naturally that the French buccaneers found themselves better treated in that port than the English filibusters or the Dutch Sea-Rovers. Almost immediately, therefore, the English drew away, and established their buccaneer base in other islands, notably Jamaica, of which island the notorious adventurer and pirate, Sir Henry Morgan, became governor.

"The steady rise of Dutch power, bringing about the Dutch War of 1665, brought about a serious menace against the English power, increased when, in 1666, France joined hands with Holland. Peace was signed in 1667. In the next thirty years, four local West Indian wars broke out, the grouping of the powers differing. All parties also sought to control the trade across the Isthmus of Panama, and there was great rivalry in the slave trade. During this period, privateers and buccaneers ceased to attack Spanish settlements only, and raided settlements belonging to any other country than their own. During the various short intervals of peace between these wars, the several treaties had become more and more stringent against the buccaneers. When, therefore, in 1697, the Treaty of Ryswick brought peace between England, France, Holland and Spain, it ended the period of the buccaneer."

"I don't quite see why," put in Stuart, a little puzzled.

"For this reason. The buccaneers had not only existed in spite of international law, they had even possessed a peculiar status as a favored and protected group. The treaty put an end to that protection. Sea-fighting thereafter was to be confined to the navies of the powers, and the true privateers and sea-rovers roved the seas no more."

"But how about the pirates—'Blackbeard' Teach, Capt. Kidd, 'Bloody' Roberts and all the rest?" queried Stuart.

"They were utterly different in type and habits from the buccaneers," explained Cecil. "After the Treaty of Ryswick, piracy became an international crime. A harbor belonging to one of the powers could no longer give anchorage to a pirate craft. Markets could no longer openly deal in loot and plunder.

"Those freebooters who had learned to live by pillage, and who thus had become outlaws of the sea, were compelled to find some uninhabited island for a refuge. They made their new headquarters at the Island of New Providence, one of the Bahamas. With buccaneering ended, and piracy in process of suppression by all the naval powers, the reason for Tortugas' importance was gone. It dwindled and sank until now it is a mere rocky islet with a few acres under cultivation, and that is all. I know it well. Much treasure is said to be buried there, but no one has ever found it. Don't waste your time looking for it, boy. You will keep away from this part of the world if you know what is good for you!"

With which menace, the Englishman fell silent, and Stuart felt it wiser to refrain from disturbing him. Even over a copiously filled lunch basket, the three in the boat munched, without a word exchanged.

At dusk they ran into a small cove at the easternmost end of the northern coast of Cuba, not far from Baracoa, the oldest city in Cuba and its first capital, where Columbus, Narvaez, Cortes and others of the great characters of history, played their first parts in the New World.

Under the shadow of Anvil Mountain, the motor boat ran up to a little wharf, almost completely hidden in greenery, and there Cecil and the boy landed. Stuart did not fail to observe that the motor boat engineer needed no directions as to the place of landing. Evidently this cove was familiar.

On going ashore, without a word of explanation to the boy, Cecil led the way to a small hut, not far from the beach. When, in response to a knock, the door opened, he said, in Spanish:

"Ignacio, this American boy is going to Havana. You will see that he does not get lost on the way!"

"Si, Senor," was the only reply, the fisherman—for so he appeared—evincing no surprise at the sudden appearance of Cecil at his door, nor at his abrupt command. This absence of surprise or question was the strongest possible proof of the extent of the Englishman's power, and Stuart found himself wondering to what extent this conspirator's web extended over the West Indies.

A phrase or two, when they were walking together through the jungle, after the parachute descent, had shown Stuart that the Englishman was especially well acquainted with the flora and fauna of Jamaica. He must possess powerful friends in Haiti, or he could never have reached the Citadel, to arrive at which point both Manuel and Leborge had been compelled to employ tortuous methods, even to disguise. The motor boat awaiting him in the Haitian jungle showed an uncanny knowledge of that locality. He had mentioned that he knew the Isle of Tortugas. He was evidently known on the Cuban coast. This plot, whatever it might be, was assuredly of far-reaching importance, if one of the plotters found it necessary to weave a web that embraced all the nearby islands.

"I'm glad I didn't promise not to tell about it," muttered the boy, as he watched Cecil stride away without even a word of farewell, "for I miss my guess if there isn't something brewing to make trouble for the United States."

A Cuban Rebel

Stuart stood with the supposed fisherman at the door of the hut until the throbbing of the motor boat's engine had died away in the distance. Then, American fashion, he turned to the brown-skinned occupant with an air of authority.

"Who is this man Cecil?" he asked. The phrase began boldly, but as he caught the other's glance, the last couple of words dragged.

Brown-skinned this fisherman might be, but the dark eyes were keen and appraising. Stuart, who was no fool, realized that his new host—or, was it captor?—was more than he seemed. At the same time, the boy remembered that he was in rags and that his own skin was stained brown. Yet the fisherman answered his question courteously.

"Does not the young Senor know him? Senor Cecil is an Englishman, and wealthy."

"But what does he do?" persisted Stuart.

The other shrugged his shoulders.

"Can anyone tell what wealthy Englishmen do?" he queried. "They are all a little mad."

The boy held his tongue. This evasive reply was evidence enough that he would not secure any information by questioning. Also, Stuart realized that anyone whom the Englishman trusted was not likely to be loose-mouthed.

"Senor Cecil said you were an American," the fisherman continued, "he meant by that—"

"Probably he meant that he knew I'd like to get this brown off my skin," declared Stuart, realizing that his disguise was unavailing now. "Have you any soap-weed root?"

The Cuban bent his head and motioned the boy to enter the hut. It was small and clean, but did not have the atmosphere of use. Stuart guessed that probably it was only employed as a blind and wondered how his host had come to know of the arrival of the motor boat. Then, remembering that the sound of the motor boat's engine had been heard for several moments, as it departed from the cove, he thought that perhaps the noise of the "chug-chug" would be a sufficient signal of its coming, for, surely, no other motor boats would have any reason for entering so hidden a place.

"If the young Senor will add a few drops from this bottle to the water," commented his host, "the stain will come out quicker."

Stuart stared at the man. The suggestion added to the strangeness of the situation. The presence of chemicals in a fisherman's hut tallied with the boy's general idea that this man must hold a post of some importance in the plot. But he made no comment.

While he was scrubbing himself thoroughly, so that his skin might show white once more, the fisherman prepared a simple but hearty meal. His ablutions over, Stuart sat down to the table with great readiness, for, though he had joined Cecil in a cold snack on the motor boat, the boy had passed through thirty-six hours of the most trying excitement, since his departure from Millot the morning of the day before. The food was good and plentiful, and when Stuart had stowed away all he could hold, drowsiness came over him, and his head began to nod.

"When do we go to bed?" he asked with a yawn.

The fisherman motioned to a string-bed in the corner.

"Whenever the young Senor wishes," was the reply.

"And you?"

"Did you not hear Senor Cecil say that I was to be sure you did not get lost?" He smiled. "You might have dreams, Senor, and walk in your sleep. When Senor Cecil says 'Watch!' one stays awake."

At the same time, with a deft movement, he pinioned Stuart's arms, and searched him thoroughly, taking away his revolver and pocket knife. No roughness was shown, but the searching was done in a businesslike manner, and Stuart offered no resistance. As a matter of fact, he was too sleepy, and even the bravest hero might be cowed if he were fairly dropping for weariness. Stuart obediently sought the string-bed, and, a few seconds later, was fast asleep.

It was daylight when he awoke. Breakfast was on the table and the boy did as much justice to the breakfast as he had to the supper. With rest, his spirits and energy had returned, but he was practically helpless without his revolver. Besides, on this desolate bit of beach on the eastern end of Cuba, even if he could escape from his captor, he would be marooned. Such money as the boy possessed was secreted in Cap Haitien, most of his friends lived in Western Cuba. If this fisherman were indeed to aid him to get to Havana, nothing would suit him better. All through the meal he puzzled over the fisherman's rough mode of life, and yet his perfect Spanish and courtly manners.

"If the young Senor will accompany me to the stable?" suggested his host, when the meal was over, the mild words being backed by an undertone of considerable authority. Stuart would have liked to protest, for he was feeling chipper and lively, but, just as he was about to speak, he remembered Andy's remark, on board the motor boat, about "food for fishes." Probably Cecil's allies were ready for any kind of bloodshed, and the boy judged that he would be wise to avoid trouble. He followed without a word.

The stables were of good size and well kept, out of all proportion to the hut, confirming Stuart's suspicion that a house of some pretensions was hidden in the forest nearby. A fairly good horse was hitched to a stoutly-built light cart and the journey began. The driver took a rarely traveled trail, but, at one point, an opening in the trees showed a snug little town nestling by a landlocked harbor of unusual beauty.

"What place is that?" queried Stuart, though not expecting a response.

To his surprise, the driver answered promptly.

"That, Senor," he said, "is Baracoa, the oldest town in Cuba, and the only one that tourists seldom visit."

Whereupon, breaking a long silence, Vellano—for so he had given his name to Stuart—proceeded to tell the early history of Eastern Cuba with a wealth of imagery and a sense of romance that held the boy spellbound. He told of the peaceful Arawaks, the aboriginal inhabitants of the Greater Antilles, agriculturists and eaters of the cassava plant, growers and weavers of cotton, even workers of gold. He told of the invasion of the meat-eating and cannibal Caribs from the Lesser Antilles, of the wars between the Arawaks and Caribs, and of the hostility between the two races when Columbus first landed on the island. He told of the enslavement of the peaceful Arawaks by the Spaniards, and of the savage massacres by Caribs upon the earliest Spanish settlements.

From that point Vellano broke into a song of praise of the gallantry of the early Spanish adventurers and conquerors, the conquistadores of the West Indies, who carried the two banners of "Christianity" and "Civilization" to the islands of the Caribbean Sea. He lamented the going of the Spaniards, took occasion to fling reproach at France for her maladministration and loss of Haiti, and, as Stuart was careful to observe, he praised England and Holland as colonizing countries as heartily as he condemned the United States for her ignorance of colonization problems.

This fitted in exactly with Stuart's opinion of the plot of which Cecil was the head. Here, in Vellano, was an underling—or another conspirator, as it might be—favorable to England, resentful of the United States, and probably in a spirit of revolt against existing conditions in his own country. The boy decided to test this out by bringing up the subject a little later in the journey.

Presently the road turned to the westward, following the valley of the Toa River. Duala, Bernardo and Morales were passed, the road climbing all the time, the mountain ranges of Santa de Moa and Santa Verde rising sentinel-like on either side. The trail was obviously one for the saddle rather than for a cart, but Stuart rightly guessed that Vellano was afraid that his captive might escape if he had a separate mount.

They stayed that night at a small, but well-kept house, hidden in the forests. The owner seemed to be a simple guarijo or cultivator, but was very hospitable. Yet, when Stuart, tossing restlessly in the night, chanced to open his eyes, he saw the guarijo sitting near his bed, smoking cigarettes, and evidently wide awake and watching. It was clear that he was keeping guard while Vellano slept. Certainly, the Englishman had no need to complain that his orders were unheeded!

Taking up the way, next morning, the road became little more than a trail, through forests as dense as the Haitian jungle. The guarijo walked ahead of them with his machete, clearing away the undergrowth sufficiently for the horse and cart to get through. From time to time, Velanno took his place with the machete and the guarijo sat beside the boy. Never for a moment was Stuart left alone.

It was a wild drive. The trail threaded its way between great Ceiba trees, looming weird and gigantic with their buttressed trunks, all knotted and entwined with hanging lianas and curiously hung with air plants dropping from the branches. Gay-colored birds flashed in the patches of sunlight that filtered through the trees. The Cuban boa-constrictor or Maja, big and cowardly, wound its great length away, and the air was full of the rich—and not always pleasant—insect life characteristic of the Cuban eastern forests.

Approaching San Juan de la Caridad, the trail widened. Machete work being no longer necessary, the guarijo was enabled to return, which he did with scarcely more than an "adios" to Vellano.

The trail now skirted the edges of deep ravines and hung dizzily on the borders of precipices of which the sharply and deeply cut Maestra Mountains are so full. The forest was a little more open. Thanks to the information given him by Cecil during their walk through the Haitian jungle, after the parachute descent, Stuart recognized mahogany, lignum vitae, granadilla, sweet cedar, logwood, sandalwood, red sanders and scores of other hardwood trees of the highest commercial value, standing untouched. Passing an unusually fine clump of Cuban mahogany, Stuart turned to his companion with the exclamation:

"There must be millions of dollars' worth of rare woods, here!"

"Cuba is very rich," came the prompt reply, coupled with the grim comment, "but Cubans very poor."

"They are poor," agreed Stuart, "and in this part of the island they seem a lot poorer than in the Pinar plains, where I lived before. Why? Here, nine out of every ten of the guarijos we've seen, live like hogs in a sty. Most of the huts we've passed aren't fit for human beings to live in. Why is it?"

Stuart had expected, and, as it turned out, rightly, that this opening would give Vellano the opportunity to express himself on Cuban conditions as he saw them. Stuart was eager for this, for he wanted to find out where his companion stood, and hoped to find out whether he was ripe for revolt. But he was surprised at the bitterness and vehemence of the protest.

"Ah! The Rats that gnaw at the people!" Vellano cried. "The Rats that hold political jobs and grow fat! The government Rats who care for nothing except to make and collect taxes to keep the people poor! The job-holders of this political party, or that political party, or the other political party! What are they? Rats, all! Tax-Rats!

"Why do the guarijos live like hogs in a sty? The Rats ordain it. It is the taxes, all on account of the taxes. Consider! All this land you see, all undeveloped land, belonging, it may be, to only a few wealthy people, pays no tax, no tax at all. But if a man wishes to make a living, settles on the ground and begins to cultivate it, that day, yes, that hour, the owner will demand a high rent. And why will he ask this rent? Because, Young Senor, as soon as land is cultivated, the government puts a high tax on it. The Rats punish the farmers for improving the country.

"What happens? I can tell you what happens in this province of Oriente. In the province of Camaguey, too. The small farmer finds a piece of good land. He settles on it—what you Americans call 'squatting'—and, if he is wise, he says nothing to the owner. Perhaps he will not be found out for a year or two, perhaps more, but, when he is found, he must pay a big rent and the owner a big tax. Perhaps the guarijo cannot pay. Then he must go away.

"Generally he goes. In some other corner, hidden away, he finds another piece of land. He squats on that, too, hoping that the tax-Rats may not find him. He does not cultivate much land, for he may be driven off next day.

He does not build a decent house, for he may have to abandon it before the week's end.

"Suppose he does really wish to rent land, build a house and have a small plantation, and is willing to pay the rent, however high it be. Why then, Young Senor, he will learn that it will be many years before he finds out whether the man to whom he is paying the rent is really the owner of the land. And if he wishes to buy, it is worse than a lottery. In this part of the island no surveys have been made—except a circular survey with no edges marked—and land titles are all confused. Then the lawyer-Rats thrive."

"It's not like that near Havana," put in Stuart.

"Havana is not Cuba. Only three kinds of people live in Havana: the Rats, the tourists, and the people who live off the Rats and the tourists. They spend, and Cuba suffers.

"For the land tax, Senor, is not all! Nearly all the money that the government spends—that the Rats waste—comes from the tax on imports. No grain is grown in Cuba, and there is no clothing industry. All our food and all our clothes are imported, and it is the guarijo who, at the last, must pay that tax. Young Senor, did you know that, per head of population, the poor Cuban is taxed for the necessities of life imported into this island three and a half times as much as the rich American is taxed for the goods entering the United States?

"Even that is not all. Here, in Cuba, we grow sugar, tobacco, pineapples, and citrus fruit, like oranges, grapefruit and lemons. Does America, which made us a republic, help us? No, Young Senor, it hurts us, hinders us, cripples us. In Hawaii, in Porto Rico, in the southern part of the United States, live our sugar, tobacco and fruit competitors. Their products enter American markets without tax. Ours are taxed. What happens? Cuba, one of the most fertile islands of the West Indies is poor. The Cuban cultivator, who is willing to be a hard worker, gives up the fight in disgust and either tries in some way to get the dollars from the Americans who come here, or else he helps to ruin his country by getting a political job."

Stuart, listening carefully to this criticism, noticed in Vellano's voice a note of hatred whenever he used the word "American." Connecting this with his own suspicion that Cecil was head of a conspiracy against the United States and that this supposed fisherman was evidently the Englishman's tool, he asked, casually:

"Then you don't think that the United States did a good thing in freeing Cuba from Spain?" he hazarded.

To the boy's surprise, his companion burst out approvingly.

"Yes, yes, a magnificent thing! But they did not know it, and they did not know why! The Americans thought they were championing an oppressed people struggling for justice. Nothing of the sort. They took the side of one party struggling for jobs against another party struggling for jobs. But the result was magnificent. Under the last American Military Governor, Leonard Wood, Cuba advanced more in two years than she had in two centuries. When the Americans went away, though, it was worse than if they had never come. Cubans did not make Cuba a republic, Americans made Cuba a republic and then abandoned us. Of course, confusion followed. And in the revolution of 1906 and other revolutions, the Americans meddled, and yet did nothing. It is idle to deny that American influence is strong here! But what does it amount to? We are neither really free, nor really possessed."

"But what do you want?" queried Stuart. "I don't seem to understand. You don't want to be a possession of Spain, you don't want to be an American colony, and you don't want to be a republic. What do you want?"

"Do I know?" came the vehement reply. "Does anyone in Cuba know? Does anyone, anywhere, know? Remember, Young Senor, the Cuban guarijo does not feel himself to be a citizen of Cuba, as an American farmer feels himself a citizen of the United States. He has been brought up under Spanish rule, and is, himself, Spanish in feeling.

"What does he know about a republic? Unless he can get a political job for himself, unless he sees the chance to be a Rat, he cares nothing about politics, but he will fight, at any time, under any cause, for any leader who will promise him a bigger price for his sugar, his tobacco or his fruit. The World War helped him, for sugar was worth gold. But now—if the Cuban wishes to say anything to America, he must do it through the Sugar Trust, the Tobacco Trust or the Fruit Trust.

"What!" Vellano flamed out, "The United States will not answer us when we pray, nor listen when we speak? Then we will make her hear!"

Upon which, suddenly realizing that in this direct threat he might have said too much, Vellano dropped the subject. Nothing that Stuart could suggest would tempt him to say anything more.

The boy had been brought up in Cuba, and, though he had never been in this eastern part of the island, he knew that a great deal of what his companion had said was true. At the same time, he realized that Vellano had not done justice to the modern improvements in Cuba, to the extension of the railroads, the building of highways, the improvement of port facilities, the establishment of sugar refineries, the spread of foreign agricultural colonies, the improved sanitation and water supply and the development of the island under foreign capital. It was as foolish, Stuart realized, for Vellano to judge all Cuba from the wild forest-land of Oriente as it is for the casual tourist to judge the whole of Cuba from the casinos of Havana.

Cuba is not small. Averaging the width of the State of New Jersey, it stretches as far as the distance from New York to Indianapolis. Its eastern and western ends are entirely different. Originally they were two islands, now joined by a low plain caused by the rising of the sea-bottom.

Climate, soil and the character of the people vary extremely in the several provinces. High mountains alternate with low plains, dense tropical forests are bordered by wastes and desert palm-barrens. Eighty per cent of the population are Cubans—which mean Spanish and negro half-breeds with a touch of Indian blood, and of all shades of color—fifteen per cent Spanish and less than two per cent American.

Foreign colonies are numerous, though small. They are to be found in all the provinces, and exhibit these same extremes. About one-half have sunk to a desolation of misery and ruin, one-half have risen to success. As Stuart once remembered his father having said:

"I will never advise an American, with small capital, to come to Cuba. If he will devote the same amount of work to a piece of land in the United States that he will have to give to the land here, he will be more prosperous, for what he may lose in the lesser fertility of the land, he will gain by the nearness of the market. There are scores of derelicts in this island who would have led happy and useful lives in the United States."

Crossing the hills—by a trail which threatened to shake the cart to pieces at every jolt—the two travelers reached Palenquito, and thence descended by a comparatively good road to Vesa Grande and on to Rio Seco. A mile or so out of the town, Stuart saw the gleaming lines of the railway and realized that this was to be the end of the long drive.

"I have no money for a trip to Havana!" he remarked.

"That is a pity," answered Vellano gravely, who, since he had searched the boy's pockets, knew that only a few dollars were to be found therein, "but Senor Cecil said you were to go to Havana. Therefore, you will go."

There seemed no reply to this, but Stuart noted that, at the station, the supposed fisherman produced money enough for two tickets.

"Are you coming, too?" queried Stuart, in surprise.

"Senor Cecil said that I was to see that you did not get lost on the way," came the quiet answer.

Certainly, Stuart thought, the Englishman's word was a word of power.

From Rio Seco, the train passed at first through heavy tropical forests, such as those in the depths of which Vellano and Stuart had just driven, but these were thinned near the railroad by lumbering operations. The main line was joined a little distance west of Guantanamo. Thence they traveled over the high plateau land of Central Oriente and Camaguey, on which many foreign colonies have settled, the train only occasionally touching the woeful palm barrens which stretch down from the northern coast.

Vellano, who seemed singularly well informed, kept up a running fire of comment all the way, most of his utterances being colored by a resentment of existing conditions—for which he blamed the United States—and containing a vague hint of some great change to come.

At Ciego de Avila, where a stay of a couple of hours was made, Stuart's companion pointed out the famous trocha or military barrier which had been erected by the Spaniards as a protection against the movements of Cuban insurgents, and which ran straight across the whole island.

This barrier was a clearing, half-a-mile wide; a narrow-gauge railway ran along its entire length, as did also a high barbed-wire fence. Every two-thirds of a mile, small stone forts had been built. Each of these was twenty feet square, with a corrugated iron tower above, equipped with a powerful searchlight. The forts themselves were pierced with loopholes for rifle fire and the only entrance was by a door twelve feet above ground, impossible of entrance after the ladder had been drawn up from within. The forts were connected by a telephone line. They have all fallen into ruins and are half swallowed up by the jungle, while the half mile clearing is being turned into small sugar plantations.

Beyond Ciego, the train passed again through a zone of tropical forest lands and then dropped into the level plains of Santa Clara, the center of the sugar industry of Cuba. From there it bore northward toward Matanzas, through a belt of bristling pineapple fields.

One station before arriving at Havana, Stuart's companion, who showed signs of fatigue—which were not surprising since he had wakened at every stop that the train had made during the night to see that the boy did not get off—prepared to alight.

"You're not going on to Havana?" queried Stuart.

"I shall step off the train here after it has started," replied Vellano. "There will be no opportunity for you to do the same until the train stops at the capital. Senor Cecil said only that I was to see that you did not get lost on the way. He said nothing about what you should do in Havana. Possibly he has plans of his own."

The train began to move.

"Adios, Young Senor," quoth the supposed fisherman, and dropped off the train.

During the long train trip, and especially when lying awake in his berth, Stuart had plenty of time to recall the events of the four days since he first met Manuel on the streets of Cap Haitien and had offered himself as a guide to the Citadel of the Black Emperor. Much had passed since then, and this period of inaction gave the boy time to view the events in their proper perspective.

The more he thought of them, the more serious they appeared and the more Stuart became convinced that the plot was directed against United States authority in Haiti. Perhaps, also, it would attack American commercial interests in Cuba. As the train approached Havana, Stuart worked himself up into a fever of anxiety, and, the instant the train stopped, he dashed out of the carriage and into the streets feeling that he, and he alone, could save the United States from an international tragedy.

A Nose for News

Through the maze of the older streets of Havana, with their two-story houses plastered and colored in gay tints, Stuart rushed, regardlessly. He knew Havana, but, even if he had not known it, the boy's whole soul was set on getting the ear of the United States Consul. It was not until he was almost at the door of the consulate that his promise to Cecil recurred to him as a reminder that he must be watchful how he spoke.

At the door of the consulate, however, he found difficulty of admission. This was to be expected. His appearance was unprepossessing. He was still attired in the ragged clothes tied up with string, and the aged boots he had got Leon to procure for him, to complete his disguise as a Haitian boy. Moreover, while the soap-weed wash at the fisherman's hut had whitened his skin, his face and hands still retained a smoky pallor which would take some time to wear off.

In order to gain admission at all, Stuart was compelled to give some hint as to his reasons for wishing to see the consul, and, as he did not wish to divulge anything of importance to the clerk, his explanation sounded as extravagant as it was vague. His father's name would have helped him, but Stuart did not feel justified in using it. For all he knew, his father might have reasons for not wishing to be known as conducting any such investigations. This compulsion of reserve confused the lad, and it was not surprising that the clerk went into the vice-consul's office with the remark:

"There's a ragged boy out here, who passes for white, with some wild-eyed story he says he has to tell you."

"I suppose I've got to see him," said the harassed official. "Send him in!"

This introduction naturally prejudiced the vice-consul against his visitor, and Stuart's appearance did not call for confidence. Moreover, the boy's manner was against him. He was excited and resentful over his brusque treatment by the clerk. Boy-like, he exaggerated his own importance. He was bursting with his subject.

In his embarrassed eagerness to capture the vice-consul's attention and to offset the unhappy first impression of his appearance, Stuart blurted out an incoherent story about secret meetings, and buried treasure and conspiracy, and plots in Haiti, all mixed together. His patriotic utterances, though absolutely sincere, rang with a note of insincerity to an official to whom the letters "U. S." were not the "open sesame" of liberty, but endless repetitions of his daily routine.

"What wild-cat yarn is this!" came the interrupting remark.

Stuart stopped, hesitated and looked bewildered. It had not occurred to him that the consular official would not be as excited as himself. He spluttered exclamations.

"There's a Haitian, and a Cuban, and an Englishman in a conspiracy against the United States! And they meet in a haunted citadel! And one said I was to kill the other! And I got away in a parachute. And they're going to do something, revolution, I believe, and—"

Undoubtedly, if the vice-consul had been willing to listen, and patient enough to calm the boy's excitement and unravel the story, its value would have been apparent. But his skeptical manner only threw Stuart more off his balance. The vice-consul was, by temperament, a man of routine, an efficient official but lacking in imagination. Besides, it was almost the end of office hours, and the day had been hot and sultry. He was only half-willing to listen.

"Tell your story, straight, from the beginning," he snapped.

Stuart tried to collect himself a little.

"It was the night of the Full Moon," he began, dramatically. "There was a voodoo dance, and the tom-tom began to beat, and—"

This was too much!

"You've been seeing too many movies, or reading dime-novel trash," the official flung back. "Besides, this isn't the place to come to. Go and tell your troubles to the consul at Port-au-Prince."

He rang to have the boy shown out.

The next visitor to the vice-consul, who had been cooling his heels in the outer office while Stuart was vainly endeavoring to tell his story, was the Special Correspondent of a New York paper. It was his habit to drop in from time to time to see the vice-consul and to get the latest official news to be cabled to his paper.

"I wish you'd been here half-an-hour ago, Dinville, and saved me from having to listen to a blood-and-thunder yarn about pirates and plots and revolutions and the deuce knows what!" the official exclaimed petulantly.

"From that kid who just went out?" queried the newspaper man casually, nosing a story, but not wanting to seem too eager.

"Yes, the little idiot! You'd think, from the way he talked, that the West Indies was just about ready to blow up!"

His bile thus temporarily relieved, the official turned to the matter in hand, and proceeded to give out such items of happenings at the consulate as would be of interest to the general public.

The newspaper man made his stay as brief as he decently could. He wanted to trace that boy. Finding out from the clerk that the boy had come in from the east by train, and, having noted for himself that the lad was in rags, the Special Correspondent—an old-time New York reporter—felt sure that the holder of the story must be hungry and that he did not have much money. Accordingly, he searched the nearest two or three cheap restaurants, and, sure enough, found Stuart in the third one he entered.

Ordering a cup of coffee and some pastry, the reporter seated himself at Stuart's table and deftly got into conversation with him. Inventing, for the moment, a piece of news which would turn the topic to Haiti, Dinville succeeding in making the boy tell him, as though by accident, that he had recently been in Haiti.

"So!" exclaimed the reporter. "Well, you seem to be a pretty keen observer. What did you think of things in Haiti when you left?"

Stuart was flattered—as what boy would not have been—by this suggestion that his political opinions were of importance, and he gave himself all the airs of a grown-up, as he voiced his ideas. Many of them were of real value, for, unconsciously, Stuart was quoting from the material he had found in his father's papers, when he had rescued them from Hippolyte.

Dinville led him on, cautiously, tickling his vanity the while, and, before the meal was over, Stuart felt that he had found a friend. He accepted an invitation to go up to the news office, so that his recently made acquaintance might take some notes of his ideas.

The news-gatherer had not been a reporter for nothing, and, before ten minutes had passed Stuart suddenly realized that he was on the verge of telling the entire story, even to those things which he knew must be held back. Cecil's warning recurred to him, and he pulled up short.

"I guess I hadn't better say any more," he declared, suddenly, and wondered how much he had betrayed himself into telling.

Persuasion and further flattery failed, and the newspaper man saw that he must change his tactics.

"You were willing enough to talk to the vice-consul," he suggested.

"Yes, but I wasn't going to tell him everything, either,' the boy retorted.

"You're not afraid to?"

Stuart's square chin protruded in its aggressive fashion.

"Afraid!" he declared contemptuously. Then he paused, and continued, more slowly, "Well, in a way, maybe I am afraid. I don't know all I've got hold of. Why—it might sure enough bring on War!"

Once on his guard, Stuart was as unyielding as granite. He feared he had said too much already. The reporter, shrewdly, suggested that some of Stuart's political ideas might be saleable newspaper material, handed him a pencil and some copy-paper.

The boy, again flattered by this subtle suggestion that he was a natural-born writer, covered sheet after sheet of the paper. Dinville read it, corrected a few minor mistakes here and there, counted the words, and taking some money from his pocket, counted out a couple of bills and pushed them over to the boy.

"What's this for?" asked Stuart.

"For the story!" answered the reporter in well-simulated surprise. "Regular space rates, six dollars a column. I'm not allowed to give more, if that's what you mean."

"Oh, no!" was the surprised reply. "I just meant—I was ready to do that for nothing."

"What for?" replied his new friend. "Why shouldn't you be paid for it, just as well as anyone else? Come in tomorrow, maybe we can dope out some other story together."

A little more urging satisfied the rest of Stuart's scruples and he walked out from the office into the streets of Havana tingling with pleasure to his very toes. This was the first money he had ever earned and it fired him with enthusiasm to become a writer.

As soon as he had left, the reporter looked over the sheets of copy-paper, covered with writing in a boyish hand.

"Not so bad," he mused. "The kid may be able to write some day," and—dropped the sheets into the waste-paper basket.

Why had he paid for them, then? Dinville knew what he was about.

He reached for a sheet of copy-paper and wrote the following dispatch—

WHALE - OF - BIG - STORY. - INFORMANT - A - KID. - WORTH - SENDING - KID - NEW - YORK - PAPER'S - EXPENSE - IF - AUTHORIZED. - DINVILLE.

He filed it in the cable office without delay.

Before midnight he got a reply.

IF - KID - HAS - THE - GOODS - SEND - NEW - YORK - AT - ONCE.

"Here," said Dinville aloud, as he read the cablegram, "is where Little Willie was a wise guy in buying that kid's story. He'll land in here tomorrow like a bear going to a honey-tree."

His diagnosis was correct to the letter. Early the next morning Stuart came bursting in, full of importance. He had spruced up a little, though the four dollars he had got from Dinville the night before was not sufficient for new clothes.

"Say," he said, the minute he entered the office, "Mr. Dinville, I've got a corker!"

"So?" queried the reporter, lighting a cigar and putting his feet on the desk in comfortable attitude for listening. "Fire away!"

With avid enthusiasm, Stuart plunged into a wild and woolly yarn which would have been looked upon with suspicion by the editor of a blood-and-thunder twenty-five-cent series.

The reporter cut him off abruptly.

"Kid," he said dryly, "the newspaper game is on the level. I don't say that you don't have to give a twist to a story, every once in a while, so that it'll be interesting, but it's got to be news.

"Get this into your skull if you're ever going to be a newspaper man: Every story you write has got to have happened, actually happened, to somebody, somewhere, at some place, at a certain time, for some reason. If it hasn't, it isn't a newspaper story. What's more, it must be either unusual or important, or it hasn't any value. Again, it must have happened recently, or it isn't news. And there's another rule. One big story is worth more than a lot of small ones.

"Now, look here. You've got a big story, a real news story, up your sleeve. It happened to you. It occurred at an unusual place. It has only just happened. It's of big importance. And the why seems to be a mystery. If you were a A Number One newspaper man, it would be your job to get on the trail of that story and run it down."

And then the reporter conceived the idea of playing on Stuart's sense of patriotism.

"That way," he went on, "it happens that there's no class of people that does more for its country than the newspaper men. They show up the crooks, and they can point out praise when public praise is due. They expose the grafters and help to elect the right man to office. They root out public evils and push reform measures through. They're Democracy, in type."

The words fanned the fire of Stuart's enthusiasm for a newspaper career.

"Yes," he said, excitedly, "yes, I can see that!"

"Take this story of yours—this plot that you speak about and are afraid to tell. You think it's planned against the United States'?"

"I'm sure it is!"

"Well, how are you going to run it down? How are you going to get all the facts in the case? Who can you trust to help you in this? Where are you going to get all the money that it will take? Why, Kid, if these conspirators you talk of have anything big up their sleeve, they could buy people right and left to put you off the track and you'd never get anywhere! On your own showing, they've just plumped you down here in Havana, where there's nothing doing."

"They sure have," admitted Stuart ruefully.

"Of course they have. Now, if you had one of the big American newspapers backing you up, one that you could put confidence in, it would be just as if you had the United States back of you, and you'd be part and parcel of that big power which is the trumpet-voice of Democracy from the Atlantic to the Pacific—the Press!"

The boy's eyes began to glisten with eagerness. Every word was striking home.

"But how could I do that?"

"You don't have to. It's already done!"

Stuart stared at his friend, in bewilderment.

"See here," he said, and he threw the cablegram on the table. "That paper is willing to pay any price for a big story, if it can be proved authentic. Proved, mind you, documents and all the rest of it. I cabled them to know if they wanted to see you, and, if they found what you had was the real goods, whether they would stake you. They cabled back, right away, that you were to go up there."

"Up where?"

"N'York."

"But I haven't money enough to go to New York!" protested Stuart.

"Who said anything about money? That's up to the paper. Your expenses both ways, and your expenses while you're in N'York, will all be paid."

"Are you sure?"

"Seeing that I'll pay your trip up there myself, and charge it up on my own expense account, of course I'm sure. There's a boat going tomorrow."

"But you couldn't get a berth for tomorrow," protested Stuart, though he was weakening. He had never been to New York, and the idea of a voyage there, with his fare and all his expenses paid, tempted him. Besides, as the reporter had suggested, it would be almost impossible for him to continue the quest of Manuel, Leborge and Cecil alone. More than that, the boy felt that, if he could get a big metropolitan paper to back him, he would be in a position to find and rescue his father.

"Can't get a berth? Watch me!" said the reporter, who was anxious to impress upon the lad the importance of the press. And, sure enough, he came back an hour later, with a berth arranged for Stuart in the morrow's steamer. He also advanced money enough to the boy for a complete outfit of clothes. An afternoon spent in a Turkish bath restored to the erstwhile disguised lad his formerly white skin.

One sea-voyage is very much like another. Stuart made several acquaintances on board, one of them a Jamaican, and from his traveling companion, Stuart learned indirectly that Great Britain's plan of welding her West India possessions into a single colony was still a live issue. The boy, himself, remembering how easily he had been pumped by Dinville, was careful not to say a word about the purpose of his trip.

Thanks to Dinville's exact instructions, Stuart found the newspaper office without difficulty. The minute he stepped out of the elevator and on the floor, a driving expectancy possessed him. The disorderliness, the sense of tension, the combination of patient waiting and driving speed, the distant and yet perceptible smell of type metal and printers' ink, in short, the atmosphere of a newspaper, struck him with a sense of desire.

Although Stuart's instructions were to see the Managing Editor, the young fellow who came out to see what he wanted, brought him up to the City Editor's desk. The latter looked up quickly.

"Are you the boy Dinville cabled about?"

"Yes, sir," the boy answered. Here, though the City Editor was ten times more commanding a personality than the vice-consul, the boy felt more at ease.

"Ever do any reporting?"

"No, sir."

"What's this story? Just the main facts!"

"Are you Mr. —" the boy mentioned the name of the Managing Editor.

"I'll act for him," said the City Editor promptly.

Stuart's square chin went out.

"I came up to see him personally," he answered.

The City Editor knew men.

"That's the way to get an interview, my son," he said. "All right, I'll take you in to the Chief. If things don't go your way, come and see me before you go. I might try you on space, just to see how you shape. Dinville generally knows what he's talking about."

Stuart thanked him, and very gratefully, for he realized that the curt manner was merely that of an excessively busy man with a thousand things on his mind. A moment later, he found himself in the shut-in office of the Managing Editor.

"You are a youngster," he said with a cordial smile, emphasizing the verb, and shaking hands with the boy. "Well, that's the time to begin. Now, Lad, I've time enough to hear all that you've got to say that is important, and I haven't a second to listen to any frills. Tell everything that you think you have a right to tell and begin at the beginning."

During the voyage from Havana, Stuart had rehearsed this scene. He did not want to make the same mistake that he had made with the vice-consul, and he told his story as clearly as he could, bearing in mind the "Who," "What," "Why," "When" and "Where" of Dinville's advice.

The Managing Editor nodded approvingly.

"I think," he said reflectively, "you may develop the news sense. Of course, you've told a good deal of stuff which is quite immaterial, and, likely enough, some of the good bits you've left out. That's to be expected. It takes a great many years of training to make a first-class reporter.

"Now, let me see if I can guess a little nearer to the truth of this plot than you did.

"You say that the only three phrases you can be sure that you heard were 'Mole St. Nicholas,' 'naval base' and 'Panama.' That isn't much. Yet I think it is fairly clear, at that. The Mole St. Nicholas is a harbor in the north of Haiti which would make a wonderful naval base—in fact, there has already been some underground talk about it—and such a naval base would be mighty close to the Panama Canal. Suppose we start with the theory that this is what your conspirator chaps have in mind.

"Now, my boy, we have to find out some explanation for the meeting in so remote a place as the Citadel. Those three men wouldn't have gone to all that trouble and risked all that chance of being discovered and exposed unless there were some astonishingly important reasons. What can these be? Well, if we are right in thinking that a naval base is what these fellows are after, it is sure that they would need a hinterland of country behind it. The Mole St. Nicholas, as I remember, is at the end of a peninsula formed by a range of mountains, the key to which is La Ferrière. So, to make themselves safe, they would need to control both at the same time. Hence the necessity of knowing exactly the defensive position of the Citadel. How does that sound to you?"

"I'd never thought of it, sir," said Stuart, "but the way you put it, just must be right. I was an idiot not to think of it myself."

"Age and experience count for something, Youngster," said the Managing Editor, smiling. "Don't start off by thinking that you ought to know as much as trained men."

Stuart flushed at the rebuke, for he saw that it was just.

"Now," continued the Editor, pursuing his train of thought, "we have to consider the personalities of the conspirators. You'll find, Stuart, if you go into newspaper work, that one of the first things to do in any big story, is to estimate, as closely as you can, the character of the men or women who are acting in it. Newspaper work doesn't deal with cold facts, like science, but with humanity, and humans act in queer ways, sometimes. A good reporter has got to be a bit of a detective and a good deal of a psychologist. He's got to have an idea how the cat is going to jump, in order to catch him on the jump.

"Now, so far, we know that the conspirators are at least three in number. There may be more, but we know of three. One is a Haitian negro politician. One is a Cuban, who, from your description, seems to be a large-scale crook. One is an Englishman, and, in your judgment, he is of a different type from the other two. Yet the fact that he seems to possess an agent on the eastern shore of Cuba—which, don't forget, faces the Mole St. Nicholas—seems to suggest that he's deep in the plot."

He puffed his pipe for a moment or two, and then continued,

"Now, there are two powerful forces working underground in the West Indies. One is the Spanish and negro combination, which desires to shake off all the British, French and Dutch possessions, and to create a Creole Empire of the Islands. The other is an English plan, to weld all the British islands in the West Indies into a single Confederation and to buy as many of the smaller isles from France and Holland as may seem possible. Both are hostile to the extension of American power in the Gulf of Mexico. Possibly, some European power is back of this plot. A foreign naval base in the Mole St. Nicholas would be a menace to us, and one on which Washington would not look very kindly.

"So you see, Youngster, if such a thing as this were possible, it would be a big story, and one that ought to be followed up very closely."

"That's what Dinville seemed to think, sir," interposed the boy, "and I told him I didn't have the money."

"Nor have you the experience," added the Editor, dryly. "Money isn't any good, if you don't know how to use it."

He pondered for a moment.

"I can't buy the information from you," he said, "because, so far, the story isn't in shape to use, and I don't know when I will be able to use it. Yet I do want to have an option on the first scoop on the story. You know what a scoop is?"

"No, sir."

"A 'scoop' or a 'beat' means that one paper gets hold of a big story before any other paper has it. It is like a journalistic triumph, if you like, and a paper which gets 'scoops,' by that very fact, shows itself more wide awake than its competitors.

"Now, see here, Stuart. Suppose I agree to pay you a thousand dollars for the exclusive rights to all that you find out about the story, at what time it is ready for publication, and that I agree to put that thousand dollars to your account for you to draw on for expenses. How about that?"

Stuart was taken aback. He fairly stuttered,

"Why—sir, I—I—"

The Editor smiled at the boy's excited delight.

"You agree?"

"Oh, yes, sir!"

There was no mistaking the enthusiasm of the response.

"Very good. Then, in addition to that, I'll pass the word that you're to be put on the list for correspondence stuff. I'm not playing any favorites, you understand! Whatever you send in will be used or thrown out, according to its merits. And you'll be paid at the regular space rates, six dollars a column. All I promise is that you shall have a look in."

"But that's—that's great!"

"It's just a chance to show what you can do. If there's any stuff in you at all, here is an opportunity for you to become a high-grade newspaper man."

"Then I'm really on the staff!" cried the boy, "I'm really and truly a journalist?"

The Managing Editor nodded.

"Yes, if you like the word," he said, "make good, and you'll be really and truly a journalist."

THE POISON TREES

For a couple of days, Stuart wandered about New York, partly sight-seeing and partly on assignments in company with some of the reporters of the paper. The City Editor wanted to determine whether the boy had any natural aptitude for newspaper work. So Stuart chased around one day with the man on the "police court run," another day he did "hotels" and scored by securing an interview with a noted visitor for whom the regular reporter had not time to wait. The boy was too young, of course, to be sent on any assignments by himself, but one of the older men took a fancy to the lad and took him along a couple of times, when on a big story.

Just a week later, on coming in to the office, Stuart was told that the Managing Editor wanted to see him. As this was the summons for which he had been waiting, Stuart obeyed with alacrity. The Managing Editor did not motion him to a a chair, as before, so the boy stood.

"First of all, Garfield—" and the boy noticed the use of the surname—"I want to tell you that your father is safe. We've been keeping the wires hot to Port-au-Prince and have found out that some one resembling the description you gave me of your father commandeered a sailing skiff at a small place near Jacamel and set off westward. Two days afterward, he landed at Guantanamo and registered at a hotel as 'James Garfield.' He stayed there two days and then took the train for Havana. So you don't need to worry over that, any more."

"Thank you, sir," answered the boy, relieved, "I'm mighty glad to know."

"Now," continued the Editor, "let us return to this question for which we brought you here. According to your story, you heard the conspirators say that their plans would be ready for fulfillment next spring."

"Yes, sir," the boy agreed, "Leborge said that."

"Good. Then there is no immediate need of pressing the case too closely. It will be better to let the plans mature a little. A mere plot doesn't mean much. News value comes in action. When something actually happens, then, knowing what lies behind it, the story becomes big.

"What we really want to find out is whether this plot—as it seems to be—is just a matter between two or three men, or if it is widely spread over all the islands of the West Indies. You're too young, as yet, for anything like regular newspaper work, but the fact that you're not much more than a youngster might be turned to advantage. No one would suspect that you were in quest of political information.

"So I'm going to suggest that you make a fairly complete tour of the islands, this fall and early winter, just as if you were idling around, apparently, but, at the same time, keeping your ears and your eyes open. In order to give color to your roamings, you can write us some articles on 'Social Life and the Color Line in the West Indies' as you happen to see it. First-hand impressions are always valuable, and, perhaps, the fact that you see them through a boy's eyes may give them a certain novelty and freshness. Of course, the articles will probably have to be rewritten in the office. By keeping a copy of the stuff you send, and comparing it with the way the articles appear in the paper, you'll get a fair training.

"We'll probably handle these in the Sunday Edition, and I'm going to turn you over to the Sunday Editor, to whom you'll report, in future."

He nodded pleasantly to the boy in token of dismissal.

"I wish you luck on your trip," he said, "and see that you send us in the right kind of stuff!"

Stuart thanked him heartily for his kindness, and went out, sorry that he was not going to deal with the Chief himself.

The Sunday Editor's office was a welter of confusion. As Stuart was to find out, in the years to come when he should really be a newspaper man, the Sunday Editor's job is a hard one. It is much sought, since it is day work rather than night work, but it is a wearing task. The Sunday Editor must have all the qualities of a magazine man and a newspaper man at the same time. He must also have the creative faculty.

In such departments of a modern newspaper as the City, Telegraph, Sporting, Financial, etc., the work of the reporters and editors is to chronicle and present the actual news. If nothing of vital interest has happened during the day, that is not their fault. Their work is done when the news is as well covered and as graphically told as possible.

There are no such limits in the Sunday Editor's office. He must create interest, provoke sensation, and build the various extra sections of the Sunday issue into a paper of such vital importance that every different kind of reader will find something to hold his attention. He has all the world to choose from, but he has also all the world to please. The work, too, must be done at high pressure, for the columns of a Sunday issue to be filled are scores in number, and the Sunday staff of any paper—even the biggest—is but small.

Fergus, the Sunday Editor, was a rollicking Irishman, with red hair and a tongue hung in the middle. He talked, as his ancestors fought, all in a hurry. He was a whirlwind for praise, but a tornado for blame. His organizing capacity was marvelous, and his men liked and respected him, for they knew well that he could write rings around any one of them, in a pinch. He began as the boy entered the door,

"Ye're Stuart Garfield, eh? Ye don't look more'n about a half-pint of a man. Does the Chief think I'm startin' a kindergarten? Not that I give a hang whether ye're two or eighty-two so long as ye can write. Ye'll go first to Barbados. Steamer sails tomorrow at eight in the morning. Here's your berth. Here's a note to the cashier. Letter of instructions following. Wait at the Crown Hotel, Bridgetown, till you get it. Don't write if ye haven't anything to say. Get a story across by every mail-boat. If ye send me rot, I'll skin ye. Good luck!"

And he turned to glance over his shoulder at a copy-boy who had come in with a handful of slips, proofs and the thousand matters of the editor's daily grind.

Stuart waited two or three minutes, expecting Fergus to continue, but the Sunday Editor seemed to have forgotten his existence.

"Well, then, good-by, Mr. Fergus," said the boy, hesitatingly.

"Oh, eh? Are ye there still? Sure. Good-by, boy, good-by an' good luck to ye!"

And plunged back into his work.

There seemed nothing else for Stuart to do but to go out of the office. In the hall outside, he paused and wondered. He held in his hand the two slips of paper that Fergus had given him, and he stared down at these with bewilderment. Fergus' volley of speech, had taken him clean off his balance.

There was no doubt about the reality of these two slips of paper. One was the ticket for his berth and the other had the figures "$250" scrawled across a printed form made out to the Cashier, and it was signed "Rick Fergus."

In his uncertainty what he ought to do, Stuart went into the City Room and hunted up his friend the reporter. To him he put the causes of his confusion. The old newspaper man smiled.

"That's Rick Fergus, all over," he said. "Good thing you didn't ask him any questions! He'd have taken your head off at one bite. He's right, after all. If a reporter's any good at all, he knows himself what to do. A New York paper isn't fooling around with amateurs, generally. But, under the circumstances, I think Rick might have told you something. Let's see. How about your passport?"

"I've got one," said Stuart, "I had to have one, coming up from Cuba."

"If you're going to Barbados, you'll have to have it viséed by the British Consul."

"But that will take a week, maybe, and I've got to sail tomorrow!"

"Is that all your trouble?"

He stepped to the telephone.

"Consulate? Yes? New York Planet speaking. One of our men's got to chase down to Barbados on a story. Sending him round this afternoon. Will you be so good as to visé him through? Ever so much obliged; thanks!"

He put up the receiver and turned to the boy.

"Easy as easy, you see," he said. "The name of a big paper like this one will take you anywhere, if you use it right. Now, let's see. You'll want to go and see the Cashier. Come on down, I'll introduce you."

A word or two at the Cashier's window, and the bills for $250 were shoved across to Stuart, who pocketed them nervously. He had never seen so much money before.

"Next," said the reporter, "you'd better get hold of some copy-paper, a bunch of letter-heads and envelopes. Also some Expense Account blanks. Stop in at one of these small printing shops and have some cards printed with your name and that of the paper—here, like mine!" And he pulled out a card from his card case and gave it to the boy for a model.

Stuart was doing his best to keep up with this rapid change in his fortunes, but, despite himself, his eyes looked a bit wild. His friend the reporter saw it, and tapped him on the back.

"You haven't got any time to lose," he said. "Oh, yes, there's another thing, too. Can you handle a typewriter?"

"No," answered the boy, "at least, I never tried."

"Then you take my tip and spend some of that $250 on a portable machine and learn to handle it, on the way down to Barbados. You'll have to send all your stuff typewritten, you know. Imagine Fergus getting a screed from a staff man in longhand!"

The reporter chuckled at the thought.

"Why, I believe the old red-head would take a trip down to the West Indies just to have a chance of saying what he thought. Or, if he couldn't go, he'd blow up, and we'd be out a mighty good Sunday Editor. No, son, you've got to learn to tickle a typewriter!"

They had not been wasting time during this talk, for the reporter had taken out of his own desk the paper, letter-heads, expense account blanks and the rest and handed them over to the boy, explaining that he could easily replenish his own supply.

"Now," he suggested, "make tracks for the consulate. Stop at a printer's on your way and order some cards. Then chase back and buy yourself a portable typewriter. And, if I were you, I'd start learning it, right tonight. Then, hey! Off for the West Indies again, eh?"

"But don't I go and say good-by to the City Editor, or the Managing Editor, or anyone?"

"What for? You've got your berth, you've got your money, you're going to get your passport, and you've got your assignment. Nothing more for you to do, Son, except to get down there and deliver the goods."

He led the way out of the office and to the elevator. On reaching the street, he turned to the boy.

"There's one thing," he said, "that may help you, seeing that you're new to the work. When you get down to Barbados, drop into the office of the biggest paper there. Chum up with the boys. They'll see that you're a youngster, and they'll help you all they can. You'll find newspaper men pretty clannish, the world over. Well, good-bye, Garfield, I won't be likely to see you again before you go. I've got that Traction Swindle to cover and there's going to be a night hearing."

The boy shook hands with real emotion.

"You've been mighty good to me," he said, "it's made all the difference to my stay in New York."

"Oh! That's all right!" came the hearty reply. "Well—good luck!"

He turned down the busy street and, in a moment, was lost in the crowd.

For a moment Stuart felt a twinge of loneliness, but the afternoon was short, and he had a great deal to do. It was only by hurrying that he was able to get done all the various things that had been suggested. Despite his rush, however, the boy took time to send a cable to his father, telling of his own safety, for he had no means of knowing whether or not his father might be worrying over him also. He worked until midnight learning the principles of the typewriter and, in a poky sort of way, trying to hammer out the guide sentences given him in the Instruction Book. Next day found him again at sea.

In contrast with the riotous vegetation of the jungles of Haiti and the tropical forests of Eastern Cuba, Stuart found the country around Bridgetown, the sole harbor of Barbados, surprisingly unattractive. The city itself was active and bustling, but dirty, dusty and mean. On the other hand, the suburbs, with villas occupied by the white residents, were remarkable for their marvelous gardens.

On the outskirts of the town, and all over the island, in rows or straggling clumps which seemed to have been dropped down anywhere, Stuart saw the closely clustered huts of the negroes. These were tiny huts of pewter-gray wood, raised from the ground on a few rough stones and covered by a roof of dark shingles. They were as simple as the houses a child draws on his slate—things of two rooms, with two windows and one door. The windows had sun shutters in place of glass and there were no chimneys, for the negro housewives do their cooking out of doors in the cool of the evening. The boy noticed that, by dark, all these windows and doors were closed tightly, for the Barbadian negro sleeps in an air-tight room. He does this, ostensibly, to keep out ten-inch-long centipedes, and bats, but, in reality, to keep out "jumbies" and ghosts, of which he is much more afraid.

HIS VISION DISTORTED BY THE VENOM-VAPOR OF THE POISON TREES, THE LAND-CRABS SEEMED OF ENORMOUS SIZE AND THE NEGRO WHO CAME TO RESCUE HIM APPEARED AS AN OGRE.

HIS VISION DISTORTED BY THE VENOM-VAPOR OF THE POISON TREES, THE LAND-CRABS SEEMED OF ENORMOUS SIZE AND THE NEGRO WHO CAME TO RESCUE HIM APPEARED AS AN OGRE.

The greater part of the island seemed, to the boy, utterly unlike any place he had seen in the tropics. Around Bridgetown, and over two-thirds of the island of Barbados, there is hardly a tree. The ground rises in slow undulations, marked, like a checker-board, with sugar-cane fields. No place could seem more lacking in opportunity for adventures, yet Stuart was to learn to the contrary before long.

Acting upon the advice given him by his friend the reporter, in New York, just before leaving, Stuart seized the first opportunity to make himself known to the newspaper men of Bridgetown. He was warmly received, even welcomed, and was amazed at the ready hospitality shown him. Moreover, when he stated that he was there to do some article on "Social Life and the Color Question" for the New York Planet, he found that he had struck a subject on which anyone and everyone he met was willing to talk—as the Managing Editor no doubt had anticipated when he suggested the series to the boy.

In one respect—as almost everyone he interviewed pointed out—Barbados differs from every other of the West India Islands. It is densely populated, so densely, indeed, that there is not a piece of land suitable for cultivation which is not employed. The great ambition of the Barbadian is to own land. The spirit of loyalty to the island is incredibly strong.

This dense population and intensive cultivation has made the struggle for existence keen in Barbados. A job is a prize. This has made the Barbadian negro a race apart, hardworking and frugal. Until the building of the Panama Canal, few negroes left their island home. With the help of his newspaper friends, Stuart was able to send to his paper a fairly well-written article on the Barbadian negro. The boy was wise enough to take advice from his new friends how best to write the screed.

Moreover, he learned that there was also, on the island, a very unusual and most interesting colony of "poor whites," the descendants of English convicts who had been brought to the island in the seventeenth century. These were not criminals, but political prisoners who had fought in Monmouth's Rebellion. Pitied by the planters, despised even by the negro slaves, this small colony held itself aloof, starved, and married none but members of their own colony. They are now mere shadows of men, with puny bodies and witless minds, living in brush or wooden hovels and eating nothing but a little wild fruit and fish.

Their story made another good article for Stuart's paper, and he spent almost an entire day holding such conversation with them as he could, though their English language had so far degenerated that the boy found it hard to understand.

The colony is not far from the little village of Bathsheba, which Stuart had reached by the tramway that crosses the island. The returning tram was not due to start for a couple of hours, and so, idly, Stuart strolled southward along the beach, which, at that point, is fringed with curiously shaped rocks, forming curving bays shaded with thickets of trees which curve down to the shore. Some of these were modest-looking trees, something like apple-trees but with a longer, thinner leaf. They bore a fruit like a green apple.

The boy, tired from his walk along the soft white sand, threw himself down negligently beneath the trees, in the shade, and, finding one of the fruits fallen, close to his hand, picked it up and half decided to eat it. An inner warning bade him pause.

The day had been hot and the shade was inviting. A sour and yet not unpleasant odor was in the air. It made him sleepy, or, to speak more correctly, it made his limbs heavy, while a certain exhilaration of spirits lulled him into a false content. Soon, under these trees, on the beach near Bathsheba, Stuart passed into a languorous waking dream.

And the red land-crabs, on their stilt-like legs, crept nearer and nearer.

An hour later, one of the Barbadian negroes, coming home from his work, was met at the door of his cabin by his wife, her eyes wide with alarm.

"White pickney go along Terror Cove. No come um back."

"Fo' de sake!" came the astonished exclamation. "Best hop along, see!"

The burly negro, well-built like all his fellows, struck out along the beach. He talked to himself and shook his frizzled head as he went. His pace, which was distinctly that of hurry, betokened his disturbed mind.

"Pickney go alone here, by golly!" he declared as he traced the prints of a booted foot on the white sand and saw that they led only in one direction. "No come back! Dem debbil-trees, get um!"

He turned the corner and paused a minute at the extraordinary sight presented.

In the curve of the cove, dancing about with high, measured steps, like that of a trained carriage-horse, was the boy, his hands clutching a stout stick with which he was beating the air around him as though fighting some imaginary foe, in desperation for his life. The sand around his feet was spotted, as though with gouts of blood, by the ruddy land-crabs, and, from every direction, these repulsive carrion eaters were hastening to their prey.

They formed a horrible alliance—the "debbil-trees" and the blood-red land-crabs!

The negro broke into a run. The old instinct of the black to serve the white rose in him strongly, though his own blood ran cold as he came near the "debbil-trees."

The crabs were swarming all about the boy. Some of the most daring were clawing their way up his trousers, but Stuart seemed to have no eyes for them. With jerky strokes, as though his arms were worked by a string, he struck and slashed at the air at some imaginary enemy about the height of his waist.

As his rescuer came nearer, he could hear the boy screaming, a harsh, inhuman scream of rage and fear and madness combined. Jerky words amid the screams told of his terrors,

"They're eating me! Their claws are all around! Their eyes! Their eyes!"

But still the strokes were directed wildly at the air, and never a blow fell on the little red horrors at his feet.

"Ol' Doc, he say debbil-tree make um act that way,'' muttered the negro, as he ran, "pickney he think um crabs big as a mule!'

Stuart, fighting for his life with what his tortured imagination conceived to be gigantic monsters, saw, coming along the beach. the semblance of an ogre. The pupils of his eyes, contracted by the poison to mere pin-pricks, magnified enormously, and the negro took on the proportions of a giant.

But Stuart was a fighter. He would not run. He turned upon his new foe.

The negro, reckoning nothing of one smart blow from the stick, threw his muscular arms about the boy, held him as in a vice, and picking him up, carried him off as if he were a baby. The boy struggled and screamed but it availed him nothing.

"Pickney, he mad um sartain," announced the negro, as he strode by his own hut, "get him Ol' Doc good'n quick!"

Half walking and half running, but carrying his burden with ease, the negro hurried to a well-built house, on a height of land half a mile back from the coast. The house was surrounded by a well-kept garden, but the negro kicked the gate open without ceremony, and, still running, rushed into the house, calling,

"Mister Ol' Doc! Mister Ol' Doc!"

At his cries, one of the doors into the hall opened, and a keen-eyed man, much withered, and with a scraggly gray beard, came out. The negro did not wait for him to speak.

"Mister Ol' Doc," he said, "this pickney down by de debbil-trees, they got um sartain. You potion um quick!"

The doctor stepped aside from the door.

"Put him in there, Mark!" he directed. "Hold him, I'll be back in a minute!"

The negro threw Stuart on a cot and held him down, an easy task, now, for the boy's strength was ebbing fast.

The doctor was back in a moment, with a small phial. He dropped a few drops into the boy's mouth, then, stripping him, put an open box of ointment between himself and the negro.

"Now, Mark," he said, "rub that stuff into his body. Don't be afraid of it. Go after him as if you were grooming a horse. Put some elbow-grease into it. The ointment has got to soak in, and the skin has got to be kept warm. See, he's getting cold, now!"

The negro suited the action to the word. He rubbed with all his strength, and the ointment, concocted from some pungent herb, reddened the skin where it went in. But, a moment or two after, the redness disappeared and the bluish look of cold returned.

"Faster and harder!" cried the old doctor.

Sweat poured down from the negro's face. He ripped off jacket and shirt, and, bare to the waist, scrubbed at the boy's skin. And, if ever he stopped a moment to wipe the sweat from his forehead, the doctor cried,

"Faster and harder!"

Little by little, the reddening of the skin lasted longer, little by little the bluish tints began to go, little by little the stiffening which had begun, relaxed.

"He's coming round," cried the doctor. "Harder, now! Put your back into it, Mark!"

Nearly an hour had passed when the negro, exhausted and trembling from his exertions, sank into a chair. The doctor eyed him keenly, gave him a stiff dose from a medicine glass, and returned to his patient.

"He'll do now," he said. "In half an hour he'll feel as well as ever, and by tomorrow he'll be terribly ill."

"For de sake, Mister Ol' Doc, I got to rub um tomorrow?" pleaded the negro.

"No, not tomorrow. From now on, I've got to 'potion um,' as you put it."

He put his hand in his pocket.

"Here, Mark," he said, "is half a sovereign. That isn't for saving the boy's life, you understand, for you'd have done that any way, but for working on him as you have."

The negro pocketed the coin with a wide smile, but lingered.

"I want to see um come 'round," he explained.

As the doctor had forecast, in half an hour's time, the color flowed back into Stuart's cheeks, his breathing became normal, and, presently, he stirred and looked around.

"What—What—" he began, bewildered.

"You went to sleep under the shade of some poison-trees, manchineel trees, we call them here," the doctor explained. "Did you eat any of the fruit?"

"I—I don't know," replied Stuart, trying to remember. "I—I sort of went to sleep, that is, my body seemed to and my head didn't. And then I saw crabs coming. At first they were only small ones, then bigger ones came, and bigger, and bigger—"

He shivered and hid his face at the remembrance.

"There was nothing there except the regular red land-crabs," said the doctor, "maybe eighteen inches across, but with a body the size of your hand. Their exaggeration of size was a delirium due to poisoning."

"And the big, black ogre?"

"Was our friend Mark, here," explained the doctor, "who rescued you, first, and has saved your life by working over you, here."

Stuart held out his hand, feebly.

"I didn't know there were any trees which hurt you unless you touched them," he said.

"Plenty of them," answered the scientist. "There are over a hundred plants which give off smells or vapors which are injurious either to man or animals. Some are used by savages for arrow poisons, others for fish poisons, and some we use for medicinal drugs. Dixon records a 'gas-tree' in Africa, the essential oil of which contains chlorine and the smell of which is like the poison-gas used in the World War. And poison-ivy, in the United States, will poison some people even if they only pass close to it."

"Jes' how does a tree make a smell, Mister Ol' Doc?" queried Mark.

"That's hard to explain to you," answered the scientist, turning to the negro. "But every plant has some kind of a smell, that is, all of them have essential oils which volatilize in the air. Some, like the bay, have these oil-sacs in the leaves, some, like cinnamon, in the bark, and so on. The smell of flowers comes the same way."

"An' there is mo' kinds of debbil-trees 'an them on Terror Cove?"

"Plenty more kinds," was the answer, "though few of them are as deadly. These are famous. Lord Nelson, when a young man here in Barbados, was made very ill by drinking from a pool into which some branches of the manchineel had been thrown. In fact, he never really got over it."

"How about me, Doctor?" enquired Stuart. His face was flushing and its was evident that the semi-paralysis of the first infection was passing into a fever stage.

"It all depends whether you ate any of the fruit or not," the doctor answered. "If you didn't, you're safe. But you seem to have spent an hour in that poison-tree grove, and that gives the 'devil-trees,' as Mark calls them, plenty of time to get in their deadly work. You'll come out of it, all right, but you'll have to fight for it!"

The Hurricane

For many days Stuart lay in an alternation of fever and stupor, tormented by dreams in which visions of the red land-crabs played a terrible part, but youth and clean living were on his side, and he passed the crisis. Thereafter, in the equable climate of Barbados—one of the most healthful of the West Indies Islands—his strength began to return.

The "Ol' Doc," as he was universally known in the neighborhood, was an eccentric scientist who had spent his life in studying the plants of the West Indies. He had lived in the Antilles for over forty years and knew as much about the people as he did about the plant life.

Kindly-natured, the old botanist became greatly interested in his young patient, and, that he should not weary in enforced idleness, sent to Bridgetown for Stuart's trunk and his portable typewriter. Day by day the boy practised, and then turned his hand to writing a story of his experiences with the "debbil-trees" which story, by the way, he had to rewrite three times before his host would let him send it.

"Writing," he would say, "is like everything else in the world. You can do it quickly and well, after years of experience, but, at the beginning, you must never let a sentence pass until you are sure that you cannot phrase it better."

Moreover, as it turned out, the Ol' Doc was to be Stuart's guide in more senses than one, for when the boy casually mentioned Guy Cecil's name, the botanist twisted his head sidewise sharply.

"Eh, what? Who's that?" he asked. "What does he look like?"

Stuart gave a description, as exact as he could.

"Do you suppose he knows anything about flowers?"

"He seemed to know a lot about Jamaica orchids," the boy replied.

The botanist tapped the arm of his chair with definite, meditative taps.

"That man," he said, "has always been a mystery to me. How old would you take him to be?"

"Oh, forty or so," the boy answered.

"He has looked that age for twenty years, to my knowledge. If I didn't know better, I should believe him to have found the Fountain of Perpetual Youth which Ponce de Leon and so many other of the early Spanish adventurers sailed to the Spanish Main to find."

"But what is he?" asked Stuart, sitting forward and eager in attention.

"Who knows? He is the friend, the personal friend, of nearly every important man in the Caribbean, whether that official be British, French or Dutch; he is also regarded as a witch-master by half the black population. I have met him in the jungles, botanizing—and he is a good botanist—I have seen him suddenly appear as the owner of a sugar plantation, as a seeker for mining concessions, as a merchant, and as a hotel proprietor. I have seen him the owner of a luxurious yacht; I have met him, half-ragged, looking for a job, with every appearance of poverty and misery."

"But," cried the lad in surprise, "what can that all imply? Do you suppose he's just some sort of a conspirator, or swindler, sometimes rich and sometimes poor, according to the hauls he has made?"

"Well," said the botanist, "sometimes I have thought he is the sort of man who would have been a privateer in the old days, a 'gentleman buccaneer.' Maybe he is still, but in a different way. Sometimes, I have thought that he was attached to the Secret Service of some government."

"English?"

"Probably not," the scientist answered, "because he is too English for that. No, he is so English that I thought he must be for some other government and was just playing the English part to throw off suspicion."

"German?"

"It's not unlikely."

Whereupon Stuart remembered the guarded way in which the Managing Editor had spoken of "European Powers," and this thought of Cecil threw him back upon his quest.

"I'll soon have to be going on to Trinidad," he suggested a day or two later. "I think I'm strong enough to travel, now."

"Yes," the old botanist answered, "you're strong enough to travel, but you'd better not go just now."

"Why not?"

"Well—" the old West Indian resident cast a look at the sky, "there are a good many reasons. Unless I'm much mistaken, there's wind about, big wind, hurricane wind, maybe. I've been feeling uneasy, ever since noon yesterday. Do you see those three mares'-tail high-cirrus clouds?"

"You mean those that look like feathers, with the quills so much thicker than usual?"

"Yes, those. And you notice that those quills, as you call them, are not parallel, but all point in the same direction, like the sticks of a fan? That means a big atmospheric disturbance in that direction, and it means, too, that it must be a gyrating one. That type of cirrus clouds isn't proof of a coming hurricane, not by a good deal, but it's one of the signs. And, if it comes, the center of it is now just about where those mares'-tails are pointing."

"You're really afraid of a hurricane!" exclaimed Stuart, a little alarmed at the seriousness of the old man's manner.

"There are few things in the world of which one ought more to be afraid!" declared the old scientist dryly. "A hurricane is worse, far worse, than an earthquake, sometimes."

Stuart sat silent for a moment, then,

"Are there any more signs?" he asked.

"Yes," was the quiet answer. "Nearly all the hurricane signs are beginning to show. Look at the sea! If you'll notice, the surface is fairly glassy, showing that there is not much surface wind. Yet, in spite of that, there is a heavy, choppy, yet rolling swell coming up on the beach."

"I had noticed the roar," Stuart agreed, "one can hear it plainly from here."

"Exactly. But, if you watch for a few minutes, you'll see that the swells are not long and unbroken, as after a steady period of strong wind from any quarter, but irregular, some of the swells long, some short. That suggests that they have received their initial impulse from a hurricane, with a whirling center, the waves being whipped by gusts that change their direction constantly.

"Notice, too, how hollow our voices sound, as if there were a queer resonance in the air, rather as if we were talking inside a drum.

"You were complaining of the heat this morning, and, now, there is hardly any wind. What does that mean?

"It means that the trade wind, which keeps this island cool even in the hottest summer, has been dying down, since yesterday. Now, since the trade winds blow constantly, and are a part of the unchanging movements of the atmosphere, you can see for yourself that any disturbance of the atmosphere which is violent enough to overcome the constant current of the trade winds must be of vast size and of tremendous force.

"What can such a disturbance be? The only answer is—a hurricane.

"Then there's another reason for feeling heat. That would be if the air were unusually hazy and moist. Now, if you'll observe, during this morning and the early part of the afternoon, the air has been clear, then hazy, then clear again, and is once more hazy. That shows a rapid and violent change in the upper air.

"So far, so good. Now, in addition to observations of the clouds, the sea and the air at the surface, it helps—more, it is all-important—to check these observations by some scientific instrument which cannot lie. For this, we must use the barometer, which, as you probably know, is merely an instrument for weighing the air. When the air is heavier the barometer rises, when the air grows lighter, the barometer falls.

"Yesterday, the barometer rose very high, much higher than it would in ordinary weather. This morning, it was jumpy, showing—as the changes in the haziness of the air showed—irregular and violent movements in the upper atmosphere. It is now beginning to go down steadily, a little faster every hour. This is an almost sure sign that there is a hurricane in action somewhere, and, probably, within a few hundred miles of here.

"But tell me, Stuart, since we have been talking, have you noticed any change in the atmosphere, or in the sky."

"Well," answered the boy, hesitating, for he did not wish to seem alarmist, "it did seem to me as if there were a sort of reddish color in the sky, as if the blue were turning rusty."

"Watch it!" said the botanist, with a note of awe in his voice, "and you will see what you never have seen before!"

For a few moments he kept silence.

The rusty color gradually rose in intensity to a ruby hue and then to an angry crimson, deepening as the sun sank.

Over the sky, covered with a milky veil, which reflected this glowing color, there began to rise, in the south-west, an arch of shredded cirrus cloud, its denser surface having greater reflecting powers, seeming to give it a sharp outline against the veiled sky.

The scientist rose, consulted the barometer, and returned, looking very grave.

"It looks bad," he said. "There is not much doubt that it will strike the island."

"Take to the hurricane wing, then!" suggested Stuart, a little jestingly. In common with many Barbados houses, the botanist's dwelling was provided with a hurricane wing, a structure of heavy masonry, with only one or two narrow slits to let in air, and with a roof like a gun casemate.

There was no jest in the Old Doctor's tone, as he answered,

"I have already ordered that provisions be sent there, and that the servants be prepared to go."

This statement brought Stuart up with a jerk. In common with many people, it seemed impossible to him that he would pass through one of the great convulsions of nature. Human optimism always expects to escape a danger.

"But this is the beginning of October!" the boy protested. "I always thought hurricanes came in the summer months."

"No; August, September and October are the three worst months. That is natural, for a hurricane could not happen in the winter and even the early summer ones are not especially dangerous. But the signs of this one are troubling. Look!"

He pointed to the sea.

The rolling swell was losing its character. The water, usually either a turquoise-blue or a jade-green, was now an opaque olive-black. The waves were choppy, and threw up small heads of foam like the swirl of cross-currents in a tide-rip.

Stuart began to feel a little frightened.

"Do you really think it will come here?"

"Yes," said the botanist gravely, "I do. In fact I am sure of it. Barbados is full in the hurricane track, you know."

"But why?" queried the boy. "I've always heard of West Indian hurricanes. Do they only happen here? I don't see why they should come here more than any other place."

"Do you know why they come at all?"

Stuart thought for a moment.

"No," he answered, "I don't know that I do. I never thought anything about it. I always figured that storms just happened, somehow."

"Nothing 'just happens,'" was the stern rebuke. "Hark!"

He held up his finger for silence.

A low rumbling, sounding something like the pounding of heavy surf on a beach heard at a distance, and closely akin to the sound made by Niagara Falls, seemed to fill the air. And, across the sound, came cracks like distant pistol shots heard on a clear day.

The white arch rose slowly and just underneath it appeared an arch of darker cloud, almost black.

At the same moment, came a puff of the cool wind from the north.

"We will have it in less than two hours," said the scientist. "It is a good thing that all afternoon I have had the men and women on the place nailing the shutters tight and fastening everything that can be fastened. We may only get the edge of the hurricane, we may get the center. There is no telling. An island is not like a ship, which can direct its course so as to escape the terrible vortex of the center. We've got to stay and take it."

"But has every hurricane a center?" queried the boy, a little relieved by the thought that the storm would not come for two hours. In that time, he foolishly thought, it might have spent its force. He did not know that hurricanes possess a life of their own which endures not less than a week, and in one or two cases, as long as a month.

"You wouldn't ask whether every hurricane has a center," the scientist replied, "if you knew a little more about them. As there is nothing for us to do but wait, and as it is foolish to go to the hurricane wing until the time of danger, I might as well explain to you what a hurricane really is. Then, if you live through it—" Stuart jumped at the sudden idea of the imminent danger—"you'll be able to write to your paper about it, intelligently."

"I'd really like to know," declared Stuart, leaning forward eagerly.

"Well," said his informant, "I'll make it as simple as I can, though, I warn you, a hurricane isn't a subject that can be explained in a sentence or two.

"You know that summer and winter weather are different. You ought to be able to see that summer and winter winds are different. The difference in seasons is caused by the respective positions of the northern and southern hemispheres to the sun. The greater the heat, the greater the atmospheric changes. Hurricanes are great whirls caused by violent changes of the air. Therefore hurricanes come only in the summer."

"That's clear and easy!" declared the boy, delighted that he was able to follow the explanation.

"Now, as to why hurricanes strike here and nowhere else. I'll try and explain that, too. There is a belt of ocean, just north of and on the equator, known as the 'doldrums,' where it is nearly always calm, and very hot. There is also a belt of air running from Southern Europe to the West Indies where the north-east trade winds blow all the year round. Between this perpetual calm of the doldrums and the perpetual wind of the trades is a region of atmospheric instability.

"Now, consider conditions to the west of us. The Caribbean Sea and the Gulf of Mexico, together, form what is almost a great inland sea with the West Indian Islands as its eastern shore. The trade winds do not reach it. The Pacific winds do not reach it, for they are diverted by the high ranges of Central America. The winds from North America do not reach it, because these always turn northwards on reaching the Mississippi Valley and leave the United States by the St. Lawrence Valley.

"So, Stuart, you can see that the Caribbean Sea and the Gulf of Mexico have over them, in summer, a region of air, little disturbed by wind, not far from the Equator and which, therefore, becomes steadily heated and steadily saturated by the evaporation from the body of water below."

"Yes," agreed the boy, "I can see that."

"Very good. Now, such a steady heating of one section of air is bound to disturb the balance of the atmosphere. This disturbance, moreover, must be acted upon by the rotation of the earth. Just as all the weather in the United States comes from the west and travels eastwards, so the track of hurricane origins travels eastwards during the course of a summer.

"For this reason, West Indian hurricanes in June generally have their origin west of Jamaica, July hurricanes east of Jamaica, August hurricanes in the eastern Caribbean, September hurricanes in the Atlantic east and south of the West Indies, and October hurricanes far out to sea, perhaps even as far as half-way to the Cape Verde Islands on the shores of Africa. This hurricane which is approaching, is from the direction of East-South-East, judging from the barometer and other conditions, and probably had its cradle a thousand or more miles away."

"And it hasn't blown itself out?"

"Far from it. It is only gathering strength and violence. Not until it twists off on its track will it begin to diminish. For hurricanes follow a regular track, an invisible trail marked out for them in the sky."

"They do!"

"Yes, all of them. This track is shaped like a rounded cone, or, more often, like a boomerang, with a short arm running north-westwards to its place of turning and a long arm running northeastwards until its force is spent. The point of turning is always in the West Indies zone. As the storm is at its worst at the point of turning, it is always in the West Indies that the hurricane is most destructive.

"No matter where they start, West Indian hurricanes always sweep north-westward until they have crossed the line of the West Indies and then wheel around sharply to the north-east, skirting the United States coast. Some strike Florida. A good many run along the coast and hit Hatteras. Some never actually touch the continent at all, and only a few ever strike inland. But some part of the West Indies is hit by every one of them."

"Are they so frequent?"

"There's never a year without one or more. There have been years with five or six. Of course, some hurricanes are much more violent than others.

Their destructive character depends a good deal, too, on the place where their center passes. Thus if, at the moment of its greatest fury, the full ferocity of the whirl is expended on the ocean, not much harm is done. But if it should chance to descend upon a busy and thriving city, the loss of life will be appalling.

"Of these disastrous hurricanes, it would be fair to state that at least once in every four years, some part of the West Indies is going to suffer a disaster, and once in every twenty years there is a hurricane of such violence as to be reckoned a world calamity."

The botanist rose, took another look at the barometer, and called one of the older servants.

"Send every one into the hurricane wing," he said. "See that the storm lantern is there, filled and lighted. Tell the cook to pour a pail of water on the kitchen fire before she leaves. See, yourself, that every place is securely fastened. The rain will be here in ten minutes."

The negro, who was gray with fright, flashed a quick look of relief at the orders to seek the hurricane wing, and ran off at full speed.

"The first rain-squalls will not be bad," continued the "Old Doc," "and I like to stay out as long as I can, to watch its coming. It will be nearly dark when this one strikes us, though, and there won't be much to see."

"But what starts them, sir?" queried the boy, who had become intensely interested, since the grim phantasmagoria was unfolding itself on sea and sky before his eyes.

"As I have told you, it is the creation of a super-heated and saturated mass of air, only possible in a calm region, such as the Caribbean west of the West Indies, or the doldrum region southeast of them. Let me show you how it happens.

"A region of air, over a tropical sea, little moved by wind-currents, becomes warmer than the surrounding region of air; the air over this region becomes lighter; the lighter air rises and flows over the colder layers of surrounding air, increasing the pressure on that ring and increasing the inward flow to the warm central area where the air pressure has been diminished by the overflow aloft. The overflowing air reaches a point on the outside of the cold air area, when it again descends, and once more flows inward to the center, making a complete circuit. Do you understand so far?"

Stuart knitted his brows in perplexity.

"I—I think so, but I'm not sure," he said. "Then the barometer rose, yesterday, because we were in the cold air area, which became heavier because there was a layer of warm air on the top of it. The storm has moved westward. The cold air section has passed. The barometer is falling now because we're in the region of warm air, which is steadily rising and is therefore lighter. That shows we're nearer to the center. Is that it?"

The scientist tapped his fingers on the arm of his chair in pleased appreciation.

"Very good," he said, "you are exactly right. And, from now on, the barometer will drop suddenly, for the whirl of the wind will make a partial vacuum in the very center of the hurricane."

"But I don't see what makes it whirl," protested the boy. "If it goes up in the middle, flows over at the top and comes down at the outside and then flows into the middle again, why could it not keep on doing that all the time, until the balance was put straight again?"

"It would," the scientist agreed, "but for one thing you have forgotten."

"And what's that?"

"The rotation of the earth."

A single drop of rain fell, then another, making a splash as large as a twenty-five cent piece.

"Now see it come!" said the scientist.

As though his words had summoned it, a liquid opacity, like a piece of clouded glass, thrust itself between their eyes and the landscape. So suddenly it came that Stuart actually did not realize that this was falling rain, until, looking at the ground, he saw the earth dissolve into mud before his eyes and saw the garden turn into what seemed like the bed of a shallow river. The wind whistled with a vicious note. The squall lasted scarcely a minute, and was gone.

"That's the first," remarked the boy's informant. "We'd better get under shelter, they'll come fast and furious soon."

Passing through a low passage connecting the house with the hurricane wing, Stuart noticed that, beside the massiveness of the structure, it was braced from within.

"In case the house should fall on it," the scientist observed, noting Stuart's glances. "I've no wish to be buried alive. In any case, I keep crowbars in the wing, so that, in case of any unforeseen disaster, a breach could be made in the walls and we could get out that way."

They entered the hurricane wing. It was not as dark as Stuart had expected. The scientist, anxious to observe the storms when they should come, had built into the wall two double dead-eye windows, such as are used in the lower decks of liners and which can resist the impact of the heaviest waves.

The crimson light had gone.. The vivid sunset reflections, now thrown back from the black arch, yet gave a reddish smokiness to the livid and sickly green which showed, from time to time, beneath the underhanging masses of inky black. The sky to the north and to the south had a tortured appearance, as though some demon of a size beyond imagining were twisting the furies of the tempest in his clutch.

"You asked," said the scientist, speaking in the hurricane wing, as quietly as he had on the verandah, and paying absolutely no heed to the moaning and praying of the negroes huddled in the darkest corner, "what makes a hurricane whirl. Yet, in the heavens, you can see the skies a-twist!"

A second rain-squall struck. Thick as were the walls, they could not keep out the wailing shriek of the wind, nor the hissing of the rain, which flashed like a continuous cutting blade of steel past the windows. The hurricane wing could not rock, it was too low and solidly planted for that, but it trembled in the impact.

After a couple of minutes came a lull, and Stuart's ears were filled with the cries and howling of the frightened negroes, not a sound of which had been audible during the squall. The scientist continued his talk in an even voice, as peacefully as though he were in his study.

"You asked what could set the skies a-twist. I told you, the earth's rotation. For, Stuart, you must remember that a hurricane is not a small thing. This heated region of the air of which we have been speaking, with its outer belt of cooler air, and the descending warm air beyond, is a region certainly not less than five hundred miles in diameter and may be a great deal more.

"Now, the air, as you know, is held to the earth's surface by gravitation, but, being gaseous, it is not held as closely as if it were in a solid state. Also, there is centrifugal force to be considered. Also the fact that the earth is not round, but flattened at the poles. Also the important fact that air at the equator is more heated than at the Polar regions. All these things together keep the air in a constant commotion. The combined effect of these, in the northern hemisphere, is that air moving along the surface of the earth is deflected to the right. Thus in the case we are considering, the lower currents, approaching the heated center, do not come in equally from all directions, but are compelled to approach in spirals. This spiral action once begun increases, of itself, in power and velocity. This is a hurricane in its baby stage."

Another squall struck.

Speech again became impossible. As before, sheets of water—which bore no relation to rain, but seemed rather as though the earth were at the foot of a waterfall from which a river was leaping from on high—were hurled over the land. The shrieking of the wind had a wild and maniacal sound, the sound which Jamaicans have christened "the hell-cackle of a hurricane." This squall lasted longer, five minutes or more, and when it passed, the wind dropped somewhat, but did not die down. It raged furiously, its shriek dropped to a sullen and menacing roar.

"Such a hurricane as this," the "Ol' Doc" continued, "has taken many days to brew. Day after day the air has remained in its ominous quietude over the surface of the ocean, becoming warmer and warmer, gathering strength for its devastating career. The water vapor has risen higher and higher. Dense cumulus clouds have formed, the upper surfaces of which have caught all the sun's heat, intensifying the unstable equilibrium of the air. The powers of the tempest have grown steadily in all evil majesty of destructiveness. Day by day, then hour by hour, then minute by minute, the awful force has been generated, as steam is generated by fierce furnace fires under a ship's boilers.

"Why, Stuart, it has been figured that the air in a hurricane a hundred miles in diameter and a mile high, weighs as much as half-a-million Atlantic liners, and this incredibly huge mass is driven at twice the speed of the fastest ship afloat. In these gusts, which come with the rain squalls, the wind will rise to a velocity of a hundred and twenty miles an hour. It strikes!"

A crack of thunder deafened all, and green and violet lightning winked and flickered continuously. The hiss of the rain, the shrieking of the wind and the snapping crackle of the thunder defied speech. The heat in the hurricane wing was terrific, but Stuart shivered with cold. It was the cold of terror, the cold of helplessness, the cold of being powerless in such an awful evidence of the occasional malignity of Nature.

Between the approach of night and the closing in of the clouds, an inky darkness prevailed, though in the intervals between the outbursts of lightning, the sky had a mottled copper and green coloration, the copper being the edges of low raincloud-masses, and the green, the flying scud above.

Squall followed squall in ever-closer succession, the uproar changing constantly from the shriek of the hundred-mile wind in the squall to the dull roar of the fifty-mile wind in between. The thunder crackled, without any after-rumble, and the trembling of the ground could be felt from the pounding of the terrific waves half a mile away. Then, in a long-drawn-out descending wail, like the howl of a calling coyote, the hurricane died down to absolute stillness.

"Whew!" exclaimed Stuart, in relief. "I'm glad that's over."

"Over!" the scientist exclaimed. "The worst is to come! We're in the eye of the hurricane. Look!"

Overhead the sky was almost clear, so clear that the stars could be seen, but the whirl of air, high overhead, made them twinkle so that they seemed to be dancing in their places. To seaward, a violet glow, throbbing and pulsating, showed where the lightning was playing.

"I'm going out to see if all's safe," said the scientist. "Do you want to come?"

Stuart would have rather not. But he dared not refuse. They had hardly left the hurricane wing and got to the outside, when "Ol' Doc" sniffed.

"No," he said, "we'll go back. We're not full in the center. The edge will catch us again."

He pointed.

Not slowly this time, but with a swiftness that made it seem unreal, a shape like a large hand rose out of the night and blotted out the stars. A distant clamor could be heard, at first faintly, and then with a growing speed, like the oncoming of an express train.

"In with you, in!" cried the scientist.

They rushed through the low passage and bolted the heavy door.

Then with a crash which seemed enough to tear a world from its moorings, the opposite side of the hurricane struck, all the worse in that it came without even a preparatory breeze. The noise, the tumult, the sense of the elements unchained in all their fury was so terrible that the boy lost all sense of the passage of time. The negroes no longer moaned or prayed. A stupor of paralysis seized them.

So passed the night.

Towards morning, the painful rarefaction of the air diminished. The squalls of rain and all-devouring gusts of wind abated, and became less and less frequent.

The sky turned gray. Upon the far horizon rose again the cirrus arc, but with the dark above and the light below. Majestically it rose and spanned the sky, and, under its rim of destruction, came the sunrise in its most peaceful colors of rose and pearl-gray, sunrise upon a ravaged island.

Over three hundred persons had been killed that night, and many millions of dollars of damage done. Yet everyone in Barbados breathed relief.

The hurricane had passed.

The Lake of Pitch

Still weak from his illness after the manchineel poisoning, and exhausted as he was after a sleepless night in the grip of a hurricane, yet Stuart's first thought on leaving the hurricane wing was to get a news story to his paper. The spell of journalism was on him.

Around the "Ol' Doc's" place, the hurricane seemed to have done little damage. Not a building had fallen. Trees were stripped bare of their leaves, cane-fields laid low, but when the boy commented on this escape, the old scientist shook his head.

"I built these structures with hurricanes in view," he said. "This old place will stand like a lighthouse. But you'll find it different in the negro quarters. Alas! You will find mourning, everywhere."

At the boy's urgency the botanist agreed to lend him a horse and light carriage and bade one of the negroes drive the lad to Bridgetown. A hasty breakfast was swallowed, and, before six in the morning, Stuart was on his way back across the island, his faithful typewriter beside him.

They had not gone far before the real tragedy of the hurricane began to show itself. Here was a house in splinters, and a group of people, crying, with bowed heads, told that death had been there. The fields were stripped bare. Near Corrington, a sugar factory showed a piece of broken wall as all that remained. The road had been washed away by the torrential floods.

In a small settlement, some negroes were working in a frenzy around a mass of ruined cottages, from beneath which sounded dolorous cries. The carriage stopped and both Stuart and the driver leaped out to aid. Ten minutes' work unearthed three sufferers, two but slightly hurt, the third with his leg broken. Alas! Others were not so fortunate.

Rising smoke, here and there, showed where fire had followed the hurricane. Instead of the songs of labor in the fields, nothing was to be heard but cries of distress. As the country grew more thickly settled, on the way to Bridgetown, so was the suffering more intense and the death-roll heavier. The drive, not more than twelve miles in all, took over four hours, so littered was the road with fallen trees and the debris of houses.

In the ruins of Bridgetown, Stuart met one of his newspaper friends, the news instinct still inspiring him to secure every detail of the catastrophe, though there was no newspaper office, the building being in ruins and the presses buried under an avalanche of brick.

"The wires are down, too," said this newspaper man, "if I were you, I'd chase right over to Trinidad. The mail steamer, which should have gone last night, hasn't left yet, or, at least, I don't think she has. She couldn't leave till the hurricane passed and the sea calmed down a bit. At present, we are cut off from the world. It'll take two or three days, a week, maybe, before the shore ends of the submarine cables are recovered. If you can catch that steamer, you'll be in Trinidad this evening."

"But suppose the cables are broken there, too?" suggested Stuart.

"They're not likely to be," his friend replied, "we just caught the southern end of the hurricane here—lucky we didn't get the middle!—and so Trinidad is likely to have escaped entirely. But you'll have to hurry to catch that steamer. I'll get in touch with Ol' Doc, the best way I can, and send your trunk on to you down there. Got your typewriter? That's all right, then. Write your story on the boat. Now, hurry up! Here!"

He shouted to a passing negro.

"Go down to the pier, Pierre, get a boat, any boat, and take this passenger. He's got to catch the steamer."

"Me catch um!"

And he did, though it was by the narrowest margin, for the mail steamer had steam up, and only waited until this last passenger should come aboard.

Stuart had counted on being able to enrich his account of the hurricane with personal stories from the passengers on the steamer, all of whom had been through the disaster, some on board ship and some ashore. There was no chance of this. Although a glorious day, not a soul among the passengers was on deck. All were sleeping, for all, alike, had waked and watched.

Stuart was dropping with weariness and sleep, but he remembered what the Managing Editor had said to him about a "scoop" and he thought that this might be the great opportunity of his life to make a reputation for himself on his first trip out. A well-placed half-sovereign with the deck steward brought him a cup of strong coffee every two hours, and though his mind was fogged with weariness, so vivid had been his impressions that they could not help but be thrilling.

Though one of the most richly verdant of all the West India islands, Trinidad had little beauty to Stuart, on his first sight of it. He saw it through a haze of weariness, his eyes red-rimmed through lack of sleep. The harbor is shallow, and Stuart, like other passengers, landed in a launch, but he had eyes only for one thing—the cable office. Since his only luggage consisted of a portable typewriter—his trunk having been left behind at "Ol' Doc's"—the customs' examination was brief.

At the Cable Office, Stuart learned, to his delight, that not a message had either reached the office or gone out about the Barbados hurricane. He had a scoop. He put his story on the wires, staggered across the street to the nearest hotel, threw off coat and boots and dropped upon the bed in an exhausted slumber. And, as an undercurrent to his dreams, rang the triumph song of the journalist:

"A Scoop!"

Stuart slept the clock round. It was evening again when he awoke. A wash to take the sleep out of his eyes, and down he went to see how big a dinner he could put away. But the doorman at the hotel, an East Indian, came forward to him with a telegram on a salver. The boy tore it open, and read:

"GOOD—STUFF—SEND—SOME MORE—FERGUS."

And if Stuart had been offered the Governor Generalship of all the West Indian Islands put together, he could not have been more proud.

He spent the evening interviewing some of the passengers who had come on the mail steamer the day before and who had stayed in Port of Spain and, before midnight, filed at the cable office a good "second-day story." Remembering what his friend the reporter had told him, Stuart realized that though he was still sending this matter to Fergus, as it was straight news stuff, it probably was being handled by the Night Telegraph staff. That would not help to fill Fergus' columns in the Sunday issue, and the boy realized that, no matter what live day stuff he got hold of, he must not fall behind in his series of articles on the Color Question in the West Indies.

This question—which takes on the proportions of a problem in everyone of the West Indian Islands—was very different in Trinidad than in Barbados. The peoples and languages of Trinidad are strangely mixed. Though it is an English colony, yet the language of the best families is Spanish, and the general language of the negro population is Creole French, a subvariant of that of Haiti. The boy found, too, on his first long walks in the neighborhood of Port-of-Spain, that there was a large outer settlement of East Indian coolies, and quite a number of Chinese. The English, in Trinidad, were few in number.

In his quest for interviews about the hurricane, one of the chattiest of Stuart's informants had been a Mr. James, a resident of Barbados, but whose commercial interests were mainly in Trinidad. Since, then, this gentleman evidently knew the life in both islands, his comparisons would be of value, and the following day Stuart asked him for a second interview.

"I'm starting out to my place on the Nariva Cocal," the planter replied, "going in about an hour. Very glad to have you as my guest, if you wish, and the trip will give you a good view of the island. Then we can chat on the way."

Stuart jumped at the opportunity. This was exactly what he was after, for the Nariva Cocal, with its thirteen-mile long coco-nut grove on the shore of the ocean, is famous. The boy knew, too, that this section was very difficult of access, the Nariva River forming a mixture of river, tidal creek, lagoon, mangrove swamp and marsh, hard to cross.

For some little distance out of Port-of-Spain the train passed through true tropical forests of a verdure not to be outrivaled in any part of the New World. "Here," says Treves, "is a very revel of green, a hoard, a pyramid, a piled-up cairn of green, rising aloft from an iris-blue sea. Here are the dull green of wet moss, the clear green of the parrot's wing, the green tints of old copper, of malachite, of the wild apple, the bronze-green of the beetle's back, the dead green of the autumn Nile." And these are expressed, not in plants, but in trees. The moss is waist-high, the ferns wave twenty feet overhead, the bamboo drapes a feathery fringe by every stream, the cocoa trees grow right up to the road or railroad which sweeps along as on an avenue between them, while at every crossing the white roadway is lined by the majestic sentinels of plantain, coco-nut palm and breadfruit tree.

Beyond St. Joseph, the ground became a low plain, level and monotonous, and given over to sugar-cane. Near d'Abadie, this crop gave place to cocoa, the staple of the center of the island, and this extended through Arima to Sangre Grande, the terminus of the railroad. During the trip Stuart's host had enlightened him by an exact and painstaking description of the growing of these various crops and the methods of their preparation for market.

At Sangre Grande, the railroad ended and a two-wheeled buggy was waiting. The planter ordered the East Indian driver to follow in the motor-bus which conveys passengers to Manzanilla, and took the reins himself, so as to give a place to Stuart. The road had left the level, and passed over low hills and valleys all given over to cocoa trees.

"See those bottles!" commented Mr. James, pointing to bottles daubed with paint, bunches of white feathers and similar objects hung on trees at various points of the road.

"Yes," answered Stuart, "what are they for?"

"Those are our police!" the planter explained. "This colony is well governed, but planters have had a good deal of trouble keeping the negroes from stealing. We used to engage a number of watchmen, and the police force in this part of the island was increased. It didn't do any good, you know! Stealing went on just the same.

"So my partner, down here, went and got hold of the chief Obeah-man or witch-doctor of the island—paid him a good stiff price, too—and asked him to put a charm on the plantation. He did it, and those bottles and feathers are some of the charms. We pay for having them renewed every year. It costs a tidy bit, but less than the watchmen and police did."

"And have the thefts stopped?"

"Absolutely. There hasn't been a shilling's worth of stuff touched since the obeah-man was here."

"But obeah wouldn't have any effect on East Indian coolies," objected Stuart.

"Coolies don't steal," was the terse reply, "those that are Mohammedans don't, any way. Trinidad negroes do. They're different from the Barbadian negroes, quite different. Obeah seems to be about the only thing they care about."

"I ran up against some Obeah in Haiti," remarked Stuart, "though Voodoo is stronger there."

"I never heard of much real Voodoo stuff here in the Windward Islands," the planter rejoined, "but Obeah plays a big part in negro life. And, as I was just telling you, the whites aren't above using it, sometimes."

"In Haiti," responded Stuart, "Father and I once found an Obeah sign in the road. Father, who knows a lot about those things, read it as a charm to prevent any white man going that way. I thought it was silly to pay any attention, but Father made a long detour around it. A week or so after I heard that a white trader had been driving along that road, and he drove right over the sign. Half a mile on, his horse took fright, threw him out of the buggy and he was killed."

The planter shrugged his shoulders.

"I know," he said. "It's all right to call it coincidence, but down in these islands that kind of coincidence happens a bit too often. For me, I'll throw a shilling to an Obeah-man any time I see one, and I won't play any tricks with charms if I know enough about them to keep away."

The buggy jogged along at a smart pace until the shore was reached, and then set down the beach over the hard wet sand. On the one side heaved the long rollers of the Atlantic, on the other was the continuous grove of coco-nut palms, thirteen miles long, one of the finest unbroken stretches in the entire world.

A hospitable welcome was extended to Stuart at the house of the Nariva Cocal, and, after dinner, the planter took him to the shores of the Nariva River, not more than twenty or thirty yards from the house, which, at this place, had a bank free of marsh for a distance of perhaps a couple of hundred yards.

"It was just at a place like this, but a little higher up-stream," said the planter, "that the snake story happened which Kingsley described in 'At Last.' Four girls were bathing in this river, because the surf is too heavy for sea-bathing, and one of them, who had gone into the water partly dressed, felt something clutch at her dress.

"It was a huge anaconda.

"The other three girls, with a good deal of pluck, I think, rushed into the shallow water and grabbed hold of their comrade. The snake did not let go, but the dress was torn from her body by the wrestle between the strength of the reptile and that of the four girls. I know one of the sisters quite well. She's an old woman, now, but she lives in Sangre Grande, still."

Turning from the river, Stuart and the planter strolled some distance down the knife-like sandy ridge between the ocean and the swamp. This narrow ridge, at no point a hundred yards wide and averaging less than half that, contains over 300,000 palms, and this plantation alone helps to make Trinidad one of the greatest coco-nut markets of the world.

"I notice," said Stuart, anxious to get material for his articles, "that nearly all your laborers here are East Indian coolies. Are they better than negroes?"

"They come here under different conditions," explained the planter. "The negro is free to work or not, as he chooses, but the coolie is indentured. He has to work. He earns less than the negro, but, by the time we pay his voyage and all the various obligations that we have to undertake for an indentured laborer, the coolie isn't much cheaper to us than the negro. But, while the negro can do more work in a day than the coolie, he won't. Moreover, if he feels, after a few days' work, that he has had enough of it, he just goes away. A Trinidad negro with a pound or two in his pocket won't do a tap of work until the last penny be spent. The coolie will work quietly, steadily, continuously. What is more, he saves his money. That's bringing about a deuced curious situation in Trinidad, you know.

"One of the queer things about the West Indies, as you know yourself, having lived in Cuba, is that there is really no middle class. Here, in Trinidad, there are the wealthy Spanish families and the English officials and planters. The blacks are the laborers. For many decades there has been no class between. Now, the East Indians, who came here as coolies, are beginning to follow the commercial instinct of the east, and to open small shops or to buy land. Hence the negro, who used to despise and look down on the coolie because he worked for even less money, is now finding himself subordinate to an East Indian class which has risen to be his superior. Then the East Indians have commenced rice-growing, and now are employing negroes, oversetting the old social basis.

"There's one thing, son, which few people realize in this color question in the West Indies. That is that the negro has not got the instincts of a shopkeeper. He doesn't take to trade, ever. If he gets educated, he wants at once to be a doctor, a lawyer, or, still more, a preacher. But this is a commercial age, and any race which shows itself unfitted for commerce is bound to stay the under dog, you know. Trinidad shows that, given equal conditions, the East Indian coolie will rise, the negro will not."

The following morning, Mr. James having gone over the books of the plantation with his manager, the two started back for Port-of-Spain.

"Why don't you live here, Mr. James?" asked the boy. "It's a lovely spot, in that coco-nut grove, with the sea right at your doors."

"Climate, my boy," was the answer. "I told you, on the way over here, that Trinidad is reckoned one of the most prosperous islands of the West Indies—though it really belongs more to the coast of South America than it does to the Antilles—but, if you stop to think for a moment, you'll see that the prosperity of Trinidad is due to the fact that it has a warm, moist, even climate all the year round. That's fine for cocoa and coco-nuts, but it's not good for humans. The warm moist air of Trinidad is deuced enervating. No, let me go back to Barbados. It may not be as beautiful—I'll admit that it isn't—but at least there is a north-east breeze nearly all the year round to keep me jolly cool."

The two travelers talked of various subjects, but, once more aboard the train at Sangre Grande, the question of Trinidad's wealth recurred to Stuart, and he sought further information.

"You spoke of the island as being prosperous, Mr. James," he said. "Has the Pitch Lake, discovered so many centuries ago by Sir Walter Raleigh, had anything to do with it?"

"Directly, not such a great deal, though, of course, it is a steady source of income, especially to the Crown. Asphalt is less than a twentieth part of the value of the exports of the island, so, you see, Trinidad would have been rich without that. Indirectly, of course, the Pitch Lake has been the means of attracting attention to the island, especially in earlier times. The facts that Trinidad is out of the hurricane track and off the earthquake belt have had a good deal to do with its prosperity, too, you know. My friend Cecil always declares that Trinidad and Jamaica together, the two richest of the West Indian islands, ought to run the whole cluster of Caribbean islands, just as little England runs the whole British Empire."

"Who was it said that?" asked Stuart curiously, though his heart was thumping with excitement.

"A chap I know, Cecil, Guy Cecil, sort of a globe-trotter. One of the biggest shareholders in this Pitch Lake. Funny sort of Johnny. Know him?"

"I—I think I've met him," answered the boy. "Tall, eyes a very light blue, almost colorless, speaks very correct English, fussy about his clothes and doesn't talk about himself much."

"That's the very man!" cried the planter, "I couldn't have described him better myself. Where did you meet him?"

Stuart answered non-committally and steered the subject into other channels, determining within himself that he would certainly go out to the Pitch Lake, if only with the hope of finding out something more about this mysterious Guy Cecil, whose name seemed to be cropping up everywhere.

The following day, having seen his friend the planter off on the homeward bound mail steamer, Stuart prepared for his visit to the famous Pitch Lake, though the planter had warned him that he would be disappointed.

Going by railway to Fernando, Stuart took a small steamer to La Brea, the shipping point for the asphalt, a town, which, by reason of its association with pitch, has a strange and unnatural air. The beach is covered with pieces of pitch, encrusted with sand and stones, worn by the water into the most grotesque shapes and forming so many resting-places for hundreds of pelicans. Some of these blocks of hardened asphalt had been polished by the sea until they shone like jewels of jet as large as a table, others, fringed with green seaweed, gave the shore an uncanny appearance of a sea-beach not of this earth. Unlike the universally white towns of the West Indies, La Brea is black. The impress of pitch is everywhere. The pier is caked with the pitch, the pavements are pitch, and, on the only street in the town as Stuart passed, he saw a black child, sitting on a black boulder of pitch, and playing with a black doll made of pitch.

Taking a negro boy as a guide, Stuart started for the famous deposit of asphalt, about one mile inland. The countryside leading thither was not absolutely barren, but it was scrawny and dismal. A coarse sand alternated with chunks of black asphalt. A few trees managed to find a foothold here and there, and there was sparse vegetation in patches.

There was nothing exciting, nothing momentous in the approach to the lake. Nor was there anything startling in the sight of the lake itself.

Although previously warned, Stuart could not repress an exclamation of disappointed surprise at his first view of this famous lake, the greatest deposit of natural asphalt in the world.

A circular depression, so slight that it was hard for the boy to realize that it was a depression at all, had, toward its center, a smaller flat, 115 acres in extent. There were no flames, no sulphurous steam, no smoke, no bubbling whirls of viscid matter, nothing exciting whatever. The stretch before him resembled nothing so much as mud-flat with the tide out. The dried-up bed of a large park pond, with a small island or two of green shrubbery, and some very scrawny palms around the edge would exactly represent the famous Pitch Lake of Trinidad.

Arriving at the edge, Stuart stepped on the lake with the utmost precaution, for he had read that the lake was both warm and liquid. Both were true. But the warmth was only slight, and the liquidity was so dense that, when a piece of pitch was taken out, it took several hours for the slow-moving mass to fill up the hole.

"The sensation that walking upon this substance gave," writes Treves, "was no other than that of treading upon the flank of some immense beast, some Titanic mammoth lying prostrate in a swamp. The surface was black, it was dry and minutely wrinkled like an elephant's skin, it was blood-warm, it was soft and yielded to the tread precisely as one would suppose that an acre of solid flesh would yield. The general impression was heightened by certain surface creases, where the hide seemed to be turned in as in the folds behind an elephant's ears. These skin furrows were filled with water, as if the collapsed animal was perspiring.

"The heat of the air was great, the light was almost blinding, while the shimmer upon the baked surface, added to the swaying of one's feet in soft places, gave rise to the idea that the mighty beast was still breathing, and that its many-acred flank actually moved."

The task of taking the pitch out of this lake, Stuart found to be as prosaic as the lake itself. Laborers, with picks, broke off large pieces—which showed a dull blue cleavage—while other laborers lifted the pieces on their heads—the material is light—and carried them to trucks, running on a little railroad on the surface of the lake, and pulled by a cable line.

The tracks sink into the lake, little by little, and have to be pried up and moved to a new spot every three days, but as they are specially constructed for this, the labor is trifling. The laborers work right beside the railroad trucks. It makes no difference where the ditch is dug, from which the asphalt is taken, as the hole left the night before is filled again by the following morning.

It has been estimated that this deposit alone contains over 9,000,000 tons of asphalt. It is 135 feet deep, and though enormous quantities of the stuff have been taken out, the level has not fallen more than ten feet.

In the lake are certain small islands, which move around from place to place, apparently following some little-known currents in the lower layers of the pitch.

Stuart went on to the factory, hoping to get some further information about Guy Cecil, but met with a sudden and unexpected rebuff. Not only did no one about the place seem to know the name, but they refused to admit that they recognized the description, and seemed to resent the questions.

Trying to change the subject, Stuart commenced to ask questions about where the asphalt came from, and the manager, who seemed to be a Canadian, turned on the boy, sharply.

"See here," he said, "I don't know who you are, nor where you come from. But I'll give a civil answer to a civil question. As for this Cecil, I don't know anything about him. As for where this asphalt come from, I don't know, and nobody knows. Some say it's inorganic, some say is from vegetable deposits of a long time ago, some say it's fish. The chemists are still scrapping about it. Nobody knows. Now, is there anything more?"

The manner of the response was not one to lead Stuart to further attempts. He shook his head, and with a curt farewell went back to La Brea, Fernando and Port de Spain.

At the hotel he found a telegram.

"GET—STORY—PRESENT—CONDITION—ST. PIERRE—MARTINIQUE—FERGUS."

Two days later Stuart boarded the steamer for Martinique, the Island of the Volcano.

THE MORNING OF DOOM

"Ay," said the first mate to Stuart, as they paced the bridge on the little steamer which was taking the boy to Martinique, "yonder little island is St. Lucia, maybe the most beautiful of the West Indies, though it isn't safe for folks to wander around much there."

"Why?" asked Stuart in surprise, "are the negroes mutinous?"

"No, bless ye!" the mate gave a short laugh. "Mighty nice folks in St. Lucia, though Castries, the capital, is a great fever town. It isn't the folks that are dangerous. Snakes, my bully boy, snakes! It's the home of the fer-de-lance."

"The Yellow Viper?" queried Stuart.

"The same. An' the name's a good one. It's more viperous than any other snake of the viper bunch, an' its disposition is mean and yellow right through. Ever see one?"

"No," said Stuart, "I haven't. I heard there were some in Trinidad, and there have been a few reported in Cuba. But I guess they're rare there. What do they look like?"

The mate spat freely over the side, while he gathered his powers for a description.

"If ye can think of a fish that's been a long time dead," he suggested, "an' has turned a sort of phosphorescent brown-yellow in decayin', ye'll have a general idea of the color. The head, like all the vipers, is low, flat an' triangle-shaped. The eye is a bright orange color, an' so shinin' that flashes from it look like sparks of red-yellow fire. I've never seen them at night, but folks who have, say that in the dark the eyes look like glowin' charcoal.

"If I had to take a walk through the St. Lucia woods, I'd put on armor, I would! Why, any minute, something you take for a branch, a knot of liana, a clump of fruit, a hangin' air-plant, may take life an' strike. An' that's all ye'll ever know in this world."

"There's no cure for it?"

"None. A little while after a fer-de-lance strikes, ye're as dead as if you'd been dropped in mid-Atlantic, with a shot tied to your feet."

"Maybe I'm just as glad I'm not going to land there," said Stuart, "though I guess it's one of the most famous fighting spots of the world. I read once that for a hundred and fifty years there was never a year without a battle on that island. Seven times it was held by the English and seven times by the French."

"Like enough," replied the mate. "It's owned by the English now, but Castries is a French town, through and through. But Castries sticks in my memory for a reason which means more to a deep-water sailor than any land fightin'. We were lyin' in the harbor at Castries when the Roddam came in, ay, more'n twenty years ago."

"What was the Roddam?" queried Stuart, scenting a story.

"Have ye forgotten," answered the mate in a return query, "or didn't ye ever know? Let me tell ye what the Roddam was!"

"We were lyin' right over there, in Castries Harbor, dischargin' coal—which was carried down by negro women in baskets on their heads—when we saw creep round the headland of Vigie, where you can see the old barracks from here, the shape of a steamer. She came slowly, like some wounded an' crippled critter. Clear across the bay we could hear her screw creakin,' an' her engines clankin' like they were all poundin' to pieces. What a sight she was! We looked at her, struck still ourselves an' unable to speak. They talk of a Phantom Ship, but if ever anything looked like a Phantom Steamer, the Roddam was that one.

"From funnel-rim to water-line she was grey an' ghost-like, lookin' like a boat seen in an ugly dream. Every scrap o' paint had been burned from her sides, or else was hangin' down from the bare iron like flaps o' skin. She had been flayed alive, an' she showed it. Some of her derricks were gone, the ropes charred an' the wires endin' in blobs o' melted metal. The planks of her chart-house were blackened. Her ventilators had crumpled into masses without any shape.

"Laborin' like a critter in pain, she managed to make shallow water, an' a rattle o' chain told o' the droppin' o' the anchor. After that, nothin'! There wasn't a sign o' life aboard.

"The harbor folks pulled out to take a look at the craft. As they came near, the smell o' fire an' sulphur met them. A hush, like death, seemed to hang over her. The colored boatmen quit rowin', but the harbor-master forced them on. Her ladder was still down. The harbor-master climbed aboard.

"On deck, nothin' moved. The harbor-master stepped down into grey ashes, sinkin' above his knee. With a scream he drew back. The ashes were hot, almost white-hot, below. The light surface ash flew up about him and half-suffocated him. His boot half-burned from his foot and chokin', the harbor-master staggered back to the rail for air.

"No life was to be seen, nothin' but piles o' grey ash, heaped in mounds. Ash was everywhere. From it rose a quivering heat, smellin' o' sulphur an' the Pit.

"Yet everyone couldn't be dead on this ghost-ship, for someone must ha' steered her into the harbor, an' dropped the anchor. Makin' his way along the rail, the harbor-master made his way to where he could reach the iron ladder goin' to the bridge, an' climbed it. The bridge was clear of ash, blown free by the mornin' breeze.

"The chart-house door was open. In it, lyin' across the steam steerin' wheel, was Captain Freeman, unconscious. His face was so blistered that his eyes were nearly shut. His hair was singed right down to the skull. His hands were raw an' bleedin'. His clothes were scorched into something that was black an' brittle. The harbor-master lifted him, an' laid him on the chart-house bunk."

"What others were there?"

"Pickin' his way, he got to the bow an' found the deck hand who had let down the anchor. He was blind an' his flesh was crisped and cracking.

"From below, crawled up four o' the engine-room crew. Most o' the others aboard lay dead under those heaps o' hot ash on the deck."

"What had happened?"

"This had happened. The Roddam had been through the eruption of Mont Pelée, the only ship which escaped o' the eighteen that were in the harbor. She got away only because she made port just fifty-two minutes before the eruption, an' had been ordered to the quarantine station, some distance off."

"Did you see anything of the eruption yourself?"

"We knew that somethin' had happened, even down here in St. Lucia. It turned almost as black as night for a few minutes, an' our skipper, who was ashore, said he had felt a slight earthquake. But we saw enough of it, right after."

"How?" queried Stuart.

"We had a lot o' foodstuff in our cargo, some of which was billed for Caracas. But, as soon as we heard the story, our captain told the engineer to get up full steam an' make for Fort-de-France. He knew the owners would have wanted him to go to the relief of the folks of Martinique. We got there the next day an' saw sights! Sights I can't ever forget!"

The eruption of Mont Pelée and the destruction of the town of St. Pierre, in 1902, over 30,000 people being killed in the space of three seconds, was one of the most tragic disasters of history, and the ruins of St.

Pierre are today the most astounding ruins that the world contains of so vast and terrible a calamity, outrivaling those of Pompeii.

The cataclysm did not come without warning. As early as March 23, a scientist ascended the volcano and reported that a small crater was in eruption. By the end of April, to quote from Heilprin, "vast columns of steam and ash had been and were being blown out, boiling mud was flowing from its sides and terrific rumblings came from its interior. Lurid lights hung over the crown at night-time, and lightning flashed in dazzling sheets through the cloud-world. What further warnings could any volcano give?"

On April 25, a crater broke into a small eruption, throwing out showers of rock-material, which, however, did not reach the town, distant a mile from the foot of the volcano. On May 5, an avalanche of boiling mud, many acres wide, tumbled down from the volcano, and went roaring along the bed of the Rivière Blanche at the rate of a mile a minute. A large sugar factory was engulfed and some 159 lives lost. On May 6 and 7, the sulphur fumes were so strong in the streets that horses, and even people, dropped from suffocation.

Again—what further warning could any volcano give?

There were other warnings. On April 30, light ashes had begun to fall. On May 1 an excursion was announced for the summit of Mont Pelée for those who wished to see a volcano in action, but that morning a deeper coat of ashes blanched the streets. The Jardin des Plantes—one of the richest tropical gardens of the West Indies—lay buried beneath a cap of gray and white. The heights above the city seemed snow-clad. The country roads were blocked and obliterated, and horses would neither work nor travel. Birds fell in their noiseless flight, smothered by the ash that surrounded them, or asphyxiated by poisonous vapors or gases that were being poured into the atmosphere.

"The rain of ashes never ceases," the local paper wrote on May 3. "At about half-past nine, the sun shone forth timidly. The passing of carriages is no longer heard in the streets. The wheels are muffled. Many business houses are closed to customers.... The excursion which had been organized for tomorrow morning cannot take place, the crater being absolutely inaccessible. Those who had planned to take part will be informed on what date this excursion will become possible."

On May 4 the paper wrote: "The sea is covered in patches with dead birds. Many lie asphyxiated on the roads. The cattle suffer greatly, asphyxiated by the dust of ashes. The children of the planters wander aimlessly about the courtyards, with their little donkeys, like human wrecks. They are no longer black, but white, and look as if hoar frost had formed upon them.... Desolation, aridity and eternal silence prevail over the countryside."

Next day, May 5, was the day when the mud crater opened. It was followed by an upsurging wave from the ocean, which added to the fear of the people, but which receded slowly and with little damage. On the day following, Pelée was shrouded in a heavy cloud, and ashes and cinders fell over a wide stretch of country. The surface waters had disappeared. Trees had been burned of their leaves. Yet a commission appointed to investigate the condition of the volcano made light of it, saying "the relative position of the craters and the valleys, leading towards the sea, enables the statement that the safety of St. Pierre is complete."

Wednesday, May 7, opened one of the saddest and most terrorizing of the many days that led up to the final eruption. Since four o'clock in the morning, Mont Pelée had been hoarse with its roaring, and vivid lightning flashed through its shattered clouds. Thunder rolled over its head, and lurid glares played across the smoky column which towered aloft. "Some say," says Heilprin, "that at this time it showed two fiery crater-mouths, which shone out like fire-filled blast furnaces. The volcano seemed prepared for a last effort.

"When daylight broke through the clouds and cast its softening rays over the roadstead, another picture of horror rose to the eyes. The shimmering waters of the open sea were loaded with wreckage of all kinds—islands of débris from field and forest and floating fields of pumice and jetsam. As far as the eye could reach, it saw but a field of desolation." The river of Basse-Pointe overflowed with a torrent of black water, which carried several houses away. Black rains fell.

Again, and for the last time—could a volcano give any further warning?

Yet the governor, a scientific commission, and the local paper joined in advising the inhabitants of St. Pierre not to flee the city, the article closing with the words, "Mont Pelée presents no more dangers to the inhabitants of St. Pierre than does Vesuvius to those of Naples."

Next day the governor was dead, the members of the commission were dead, the editor was dead, and the presses on which this article had been printed had, in one blast, been fused into a mass of twisted metal.

Came the 8th of May, 1902.

Shortly after midnight the thunders ceased for a while, but by four o'clock, two hours before the shadows of night had lifted, an ominous cloud was seen flowing out to sea, followed in its train by streaks of fiery cinders.

The sun was barely above the horizon when the roaring began again. The Vicar-General describes these sounds as follows: "I distinguished clearly four kinds of noises; first the clap of thunder, which followed the lightning at intervals of twenty seconds; then the mighty muffled detonations of the volcano, like the roaring of many cannon fired simultaneously; third, the continuous rumbling of the crater, which the inhabitants designated the 'roaring of the lion,' and then last, as though furnishing the bass for this gloomy music, the deep noise of the swelling waters, of all the torrents which take their source upon the mountain, generated by an overflow such as has never yet been seen. This immense rising of thirty streams at once, without one drop of water having fallen on the sea-coast, gives some idea of the cataracts which must pour down upon the summit from the storm-clouds gathered around the crater."

"Hundreds of agonized people," writes Heilprin, in his great scientific work on the catastrophe, "had gathered to their devotions in the Cathedral and the Cathedral Square, this being Ascension Day, but probably there were not many among them who did not feel that the tide of the world had turned, for even through the atmosphere of the sainted bells, the fiery missiles were being hurled to warn of destruction. The fate of the city and of its inhabitants had already been sealed.

"The big hand of the clock of the Military Hospital had just reached the minute mark of 7:50 a.m. when a great brown cloud was seen to issue from the side of the volcano, followed almost immediately by a cloud of vapory blackness, which separated from it and took a course downward to the sea. Deafening detonations from the interior preceded this appearance, and a lofty white pennant was seen to rise from the summit of the volcano.

"With wild fury the black cloud rolled down the mountain slope, pressing closely the contours of the valley along which had previously swept the mud-flow that overwhelmed the factory three days before, and spreading fan-like to the sea.

"In two minutes, or less, it had reached the doomed city, a flash of blinding intensity parted its coils, and St. Pierre was ablaze. The clock of the Military Hospital halted at 7:52 a.m.—a historic time-mark among the ruins, the recorder of one of the greatest catastrophic events that are written in the history of the world."

Just before the cloud struck, its violet-grey center showed, and the forepart of this was luminous. It struck the town with the fury of a tornado of flame. Whirls of fire writhed spirally about it. The mountain had belched death, death in many forms: death by fire, death by poisonous gases, death by a super-furnace heat, but, principally, death by a sudden suffocation, the fiery and flaming cloud having consumed all the breathable air.

Whole streets of houses were mown down by the flaming scythe. Walls three to four feet in thickness were blown away like paper. Massive machinery was crumpled up as if it had been clutched in a titanic white-hot metal hand. The town was raked by a hurricane of incandescent dust and super-heated gas.

The violet luminosity, with its writhing serpents of flame, was followed in a second or two by a thousand points of light as the town took fire, followed, almost instantaneously, by a burst of light of every color in the spectrum, as a thousand substances leaped into combustion, and then, in a moment——

Night!

An impenetrable cloud of smoke and ash absolutely blotted out the sun. The sky was covered. The hills were hidden. The sea was as invisible as at midnight. Even the grayness of the ash gave back no light; there was none to give.

Three seconds had elapsed since the violet-gray cloud of fury struck the town, but in those three seconds 30,000 people lay dead, slain with such appalling swiftness that none knew their fate. No one had tried to escape.

The eruption was witnessed, from a distance, by only one trained observer, Roger Arnoux, and a translation of his record is, in part, as follows:

"Having left St. Pierre at about five in the evening (May 7) I was witness to the following spectacle: Enormous rocks, being clearly distinguishable, were being projected from the crater to a considerable elevation, so high, indeed, as to occupy a quarter of a minute in their flight.

"About eight o'clock of the evening we recognized for the first time, playing about the crater, fixed fires that burned with a brilliant white flame. Shortly afterwards, several detonations, similar to those that had been heard at St. Pierre, were noted coming from the south, which confirmed me in my opinion that there already existed a number of submarine craters from which gases were being projected, to explode when coming in contact with the air.

"Having retired for the night, at about nine o'clock, I awoke shortly afterwards in the midst of a suffocating heat and completely bathed in perspiration.... I awoke again about eleven thirty-five, having felt a trembling of the earth ... but again went to sleep, waking at half-past seven.

My first observation was of the crater, which I found sufficiently calm, the vapors being chased swiftly under pressure of an east wind.

"At about eight o'clock, when still watching the crater (M. Arnoux was the only man who saw the beginning of the eruption and lived to tell the tale), I noted a small cloud pass out, followed two seconds after by a considerable cloud, whose flight to the Pointe de Carbet (beyond the city) occupied less than three seconds, being at the same time already in our zenith, thus showing that it developed almost as rapidly in height as in length. The vapors were of a violet-gray color and seemingly very dense, for, although endowed with an almost inconceivably powerful ascensive force, they retained to the zenith their rounded summits. Innumerable electric scintillations played through the chaos of vapors, at the same time that the ears were deafened by a frightful fracas.

"I had, at this time, an impression that St. Pierre had been destroyed.... As the monster seemed to near us, my people, panic-stricken, ran to a neighboring hillock that dominated the house, begging me to do the same.... Hardly had we arrived at the summit when the sun was completely veiled, and in its place came almost complete blackness.... At this time we observed over St. Pierre, a column of fire, estimated to be 1,200 feet in height, which seemed to be endowed with the movement of rotation as well as onward movement." St. Pierre was no more.

Rescuers were soon on their way. Twenty-three minutes after the clouds had been seen rising from Mont Pelée and the cable and telephone lines were broken, a little steamer left Fort-de-France, the capital. It reached half-way, then, finding that the rain of stones and ashes threatened to sink it, returned. The boat started anew at ten o'clock and rounded the point of Carbet. The volcano was shrouded in smoke and ashes. For three miles the coast was in flames. Seventeen vessels in the roadstead, two of which were American steamers, burned at anchor. The heat from this immense conflagration prevented the boat from proceeding and it returned to Fort-de-France, reaching there at one o'clock, bringing the sinister tidings.

At midday, the Acting Governor of Martinique ordered the Suchet to go with troops to be under the direction of the Governor, then at St. Pierre. About three o'clock, a party was landed on the shore. The pier was covered with bodies. The town was all in fire and in ruins. The heat was such that the landing party could not endure more than three or four minutes. The Governor was dead also.

"St. Pierre," writes a witness on another rescue ship, which arrived at almost the same moment, "is no more. Its ruins stretch before us, in their shroud of smoke and ashes, gloomy and silent, a city of the dead. Our eyes seek the inhabitants fleeing distracted, or returning to look for the dead. Nothing to be seen. No living soul appears in this desert of desolation, encompassed by appalling silence.... Through the clouds of ashes and of smoke diffused in our atmosphere, the sun breaks wan and dim, as it is never seen in our skies, and throws over the whole picture a sinister light, suggestive of a world beyond the grave."

Two of the inhabitants, and two only, escaped; one a negro prisoner, who was not found until three days later, burned half to death in his prison cell; and one, a shoemaker, who, by some strange eddy in the all-killing gas, and who was on the very edge of the track of destruction, fled, though others fell dead on every side of him.

A second eruption, coupled with an earthquake, on May 20, completed the wreckage of the buildings. This outburst was even more violent than the first. There was no loss of life, for no one was left to slay.

Five years later, Sir Frederick Treves visited St. Pierre. "Along the whole stretch of the bay," he writes, "there is not one living figure to be seen, not one sign of human life, not even a poor hut, nor grazing cattle.... A generous growth of jungle has spread over the place in these five years. Rank bushes, and even small trees, make a thicket along some of the less traversed ways.... Over some of the houses luxuriant creepers have spread, while long grass, ferns and forest flowers have filled up many a court and modest lane."

Twelve years later, a visitor to St. Pierre found a small wooden pier erected. A tiny hotel had been built. Huts were clustering under the ruins. Several parties were at work clearing away the ruins, but slowly, for the government of the colony would not assist in the work, believing that the region was unsafe. At the time of this visit, Mont Pelée was still smoking.

This was the ruined city which Stuart was going to see. On board the steamer were the two or three books which tell the story of the great eruption, and the boy filled his brain full of the terrible story that he might better feel the great adventure that the next day should bring him.

The steamer reached Fort-de-France in the evening, and the boy found the town, though ill-lighted, gay. A band was playing in the Plaza, not far from the landing place and most of the shops were still open. Morning showed an even brighter Fort-de-France, for, though when St. Pierre was in its glory, Fort-de-France was the lesser town, the capital now is the center of the commercial prosperity of the island. For this, however, Stuart had little regard. Sunrise found him on the little steamer which leaves daily for St. Pierre.

The journey was not long, three hours along a coast of steep cliffs with verdant mountains above. Small fishing hamlets, half-hidden behind coco-nut palms, appeared in every cove. The steamer passed Carbet, that town on the edge of the great eruptive flood, which had its own death-list, and they turned the point of land into the harbor of St. Pierre.

Before the boy's eyes rose the Mountain of Destruction, sullen, twisted, wrinkled and still menacing, not all silent yet. The hills around were green, and verdure spread over the country once deep in volcanic ash. But Mont Pelée was brown and bald still.

Nineteen years had passed since the eruption, but St. Pierre had not recovered. At first sight, from the sea, the town gave a slight impression of being rebuilt. But this was only the strange combination of old ruins and modern fishing huts. The handsome stone wharves still stood, but no vessels lay beside them.

The little steamer slowed and tied up at a tiny wooden pier. A statue, symbolical of St. Pierre in her agony, had been erected on the end of the pier. The boy landed, and walked slowly along the frail wooden structure, to take in the scene as it presented itself to him.

Alas, for St. Pierre! As Lafcadio Hearn described it—"the quaint, whimsical, wonderfully colored little town, the sweetest, queerest, darlingest little city in the Antilles.... Walls are lemon color, quaint balconies and lattices are green. Palm trees rise from courts and gardens into the warm blue sky, indescribably blue, that appears almost to touch the feathery heads of them. And all things within and without the yellow vista are steeped in a sunshine electrically white, in a radiance so powerful that it lends even to the pavement of basalt the glitter of silver ore.

"Everywhere rushes mountain water—cool and crystal—clear, washing the streets; from time to time you come to some public fountain flinging a silvery column to the sun.... And often you will note, in the course of a walk, little drinking fountains contrived in the angle of a building, or in the thick walls bordering the bulwarks or enclosing public squares; glittering threads of water spurting through lion-lips of stone."

Alas for St. Pierre!

Above the pier but one street had been partly restored, and, at every gap, the boy's gaze encountered gray ruins. The ash, poured out by the mountain in its vast upheaval, has made a rich soil. To Stuart's eyes, the town was a town of dreams, of great stone staircases that led to nowhere, of high archways that gave upon a waste. The entrance hall of the great Cathedral, once one of the finest in the West Indies, still leads to the high altar, but that finds its home in a little wooden structure with a tin roof, shrinking in what was once a corner of the apse.

Built as a lean-to in the corner of what had once been a small, but strongly-built house was a store, a very small store, outside the door of which a crippled negro was sitting. Thinking that this might be one of the old-timers of St. Pierre, Stuart stopped and bought a small trinket, partly as a memento, partly as a means of getting into conversation.

"But yes, Monsieur," answered the storekeeper, "it was my wife and I—we escaped. My wife, she had been sent into Morne Rouge, that very morning, with a message from her mistress. Me, I was working on the road, not more than a mile away. I saw nothing of it, Monsieur. About half-past seven that morning (twenty-two minutes, therefore, before the final eruption) a shower of stones fell where I was working. One fell on my back, and left me crippled, as you see. But my four children, ah! Monsieur, they sleep here, somewhere!"

He waved his hand toward the riot of ruin and foliage which now marks the city which once prided itself on being called "the gayest little city in the West Indies."

"Yet you have come back!" exclaimed Stuart.

"But yes, Monsieur, what would you? It pleased God that I should be born here, that my children should be taken away from me here; and, maybe, that I should die here, too."

"You are not afraid that Mont Pelée will begin again?"

The negro shrugged his shoulders.

"It is my home, Monsieur," he said simply. "Better a home which is sad than the place of a stranger which is gay. But we hope, Monsieur, that some day the government of Martinique will accept a parole of good conduct from the Great Eater of Lives"—he pointed to Mont Pelée—"and give us back our town again."

Next morning, studying the life of the little town, Stuart found that many others shared the view of the crippled negro. The little market-place on the Place Bertin, though lacking any shelter from pouring rain or blazing sun, was crowded with three or four hundred market women. Daily the little steamer takes a cargo from St. Pierre, for the ash from the volcano has enriched the soil, and the planters are growing wealthy. There are many more little houses and thatched huts tucked into corners of the ruins than appear at first sight, and a hotel has been built for the tourists who visit the strange spot.

The crater in Mont Pelée is silent now; the great vent which hurled white-hot rocks, incandescent dust and mephitic gases, is now covered with a thick green shrubbery, only here and there do small smoke-holes emit a light sulphurous vapor; but the great mountain, treeless, wrinkled, implacable, seemed to Stuart to throw a solemn shadow of threat upon the town. The secret of St. Pierre, as Stuart wrote to his paper, "lies in the hope of its inhabitants, but its real future lies in the parole of good conduct from the Great Eater of Human Lives, Mont Pelée."

A Corsairs Death

There is not a corner of the world which is more full of historic memories than is the West Indies. Dominica, the next island which Stuart passed after he had left Martinique, besides being one of the scenic glories of the world, described as "a tabernacle for the sun, a shrine of a thousand spires, rising tier above tier, in one exquisite fabric of green, purple and grey," has many claims to fame. Here, the cannibal Caribs were so fierce that for 255 years they defied the successive fleets of Spaniards, French and English who tried to take possession of the island. Some three hundred Caribs still dwell upon the island upon a reservation provided by the government. The warriors no longer make war, and fish has taken the place of the flesh of their enemies as a staple diet.

Under the cliffs of Dominica is a memory of the Civil War, for there the Confederate vessel Alabama finally escaped the Federal man-of-war Iroquois. A few miles further north, between Dominica and Guadeloupe, in The Saints Passage, was fought, in 1782, the great sea-battle between Rodney and De Grasse, which ended in the decisive victory of the English over the French and gave Britain the mastery of the Caribbean Sea. It ranks as one of the great historic sea-fights of the world.

The next island on the direct line to the north, St. Kitts, is not destitute of fame. As Cecil had told Stuart, St. Kitts or St. Christopher was first a home for buccaneers, and later one of the keys to the military occupation of the West Indies. Its neighbor, St. Nevis, together with other claims to romance, has a special interest to the United States in that Alexander Hamilton—perhaps one of the greatest of American statesmen—was born there.

Near St. Kitts lies Antigua, where the Most Blessed Trinity—despite her name, one of the most famous pirate craft afloat—settled after her bloody cruises. Its captain was Bartholomew Sharp, described as "an acrid-looking villain whose scarred face had been tanned to the color of old brandy, whose shaggy brows were black with gunpowder, and whose long hair, half singed off in a recent fight, was tied up in a nun's wimple. He was dressed in the long embroidered coat of a Spanish grandee, and, as there was a bullet hole in the back of the garment, it may be surmised that the previous owner had come to a violent end. His hose of white silk were as dirty as the deck, his shoe buckles were of dull silver."

Sharp, with 330 buccaneers, had left the West Indies in April, 1760. They landed on the mainland, and, crossing the isthmus, made for Panama. Having secured canoes, they attacked the Spanish fleet lying at Perico, an island off Panama City, and, after one of the most desperate fights recorded in the annals of piracy, they took all the ships, including the Most Blessed Trinity. Then followed a long record of successful piracy, of battle, murder and sudden death, of mutiny and slaughter grim and great. Sharp, who, with all his crimes, was as good a navigator as he was reckless a fighter, sailed the Most Blessed Trinity with his crew of desperadoes the whole length of South America, rounded the Horn and, after eighteen months of adventure, peril and hardship, reached the West Indies again.

"The log of the voyage," writes Treves, "affords lurid reading. It records how they landed and took towns, how they filled the little market squares with corpses, how they pillaged the churches, ransacked the houses and then committed the trembling places to the flames.

"It tells how they tortured frenzied men until, in their agony, they told of hiding places where gold was buried; how they spent an unholy Christmas at Juan Fernandez; how, in a little island cove, they fished with a greasy lead for golden pieces which Drake is believed to have thrown overboard for want of carrying room. It gives account of a cargo of sugar and wine, of tallow and hides, of bars of silver and pieces of eight, of altar chalices and ladies' trinkets, of scented laces, and of rings torn from the clenched and still warm fingers of the dead.

"The 'valiant commander' had lost many of his company on the dangerous voyage. Some had died in battle; others had mumbled out their lives in the delirium of fever, sunstroke or drink; certain poor souls, with racked joints and bleeding backs, were crouching in Spanish prisons; one had been marooned on a desert island in the Southern Pacific Ocean." At the last, Sharp turned over the ship to the remainder of his crew and set sail, rich and respected (!) for England.

On the way from St. Kitts to St. Thomas, Stuart passed the two strange islands of St. Eustatius and Saba, remnants of the once great Dutch power in the West Indies. Statia, as the first island is generally called, is a decadent spot, its commerce fallen to nothing, the warehouses along the sea-front of its only town, in ruins. Yet once, strange as it may seem, for a few brief months, Statia became the scene of a wild commercial orgy, and the place where once was held "the most stupendous auction in the history of the universe."

It happened thus: When the American Revolulutionary War broke out, England being already at war with France, commercial affairs in the West Indies became complicated by the fact that the Spanish, the French and the English, all enacted trading restrictions so stringent that practically every port in the West Indies was closed. The Dutch, seizing the opportunity, made Statia a free port. Immediately, the whole of French, English, Spanish, Dutch and American trade was thrown upon the tiny beach of Fort Oranje.

More than that, Statia became the center for contraband of war. All the other islands took advantage of this. Statia became a huge arsenal. American privateers and blockade-runners were convoyed by Dutch men-of-war, which, of course, could not be attacked. Smugglers were amply provided with Dutch papers. Goods poured in from Europe every day in the week. Rich owners of neighboring islands, not knowing how the French-English strife might turn out, sent their valuables to Statia for safe keeping. The little island became a treasure-house.

At times more than a hundred merchant vessels could be seen swinging to their anchors in the roadstead. A mushroom town appeared as by magic. Warehouses rose by scores. The beach was hidden by piles of boxes, bags and bales for which no storeroom could be found. Merchants came from all ports, especially the Jews and Levantines, who, since the beginning of time, have been the trade-rovers of the sea. Neither by day nor by night did the Babel of commerce cease. Unlike other West Indian towns, where such a condition led to gaiety and pleasure, Fort Oranje retained its Dutch character. It was a hysteria, but a hysteria of buying and selling alone.

Then, one fine day, February 3, 1781, Rodney came down with a British fleet and captured Fort Oranje and all that it contained. There were political complications involved, but Rodney bothered little about that. Fort Oranje was a menace to British power. Rodney took it without remorse, appropriated the more than $20,000,000 worth of goods lying on the beach and the warehouses, and the 150 merchantmen, which, on that day, were lying in the bay. Jews and Levantines were stripped to the skin and sent packing. The Dutch surrendered and took their medicine phlegmatically. The French, as open enemies, were allowed to depart with courtesy.

Then came the great auction. Without reserve, without remorse, over $20,000,000 worth of goods were put up for what they would fetch. Boxes, crates, bales and bags melted away like snow before the sun. Warehouses bursting with goods became but empty shells. Traders' booths were abandoned, one by one. Just for a few months the commercial debauch lasted, then Rodney sailed away. Since then, the selling on the beach of Statia has been confined to a little sugar and a few yams.

For the United States, the little fort above Fort Oranje has a historic memory. From the old cannon, still in position on that fort, was fired the first foreign salute to the Stars and Stripes, the first salute which recognized the United States as a sovereign nation.

It was on the 16th of November, 1776, that the brig Andrea Doria, fourteen guns, third of the infant American navy of five vessels, under the command of Josiah Robinson, sailed into the open roadstead of St. Eustatius, and dropped anchor almost under the guns of Fort Oranje.

"She could have chosen no more fitting name," writes Fenger, "than that of the famous townsman of Columbus.... The Andrea Doria may have attracted but little attention as she appeared in the offing ... but, with the quick eyes of seafarers, the guests of Howard's Tavern had probably left their rum for a moment to have their first glimpse of a strange flag which they all knew must be that of the new republic.

"Abraham Ravené, commandant of the fort, lowered the red-white-and-blue flag of Holland in recognition of the American ship. In return, the Andrea Doria fired a salute.

"This put the commandant in a quandary. Anchored not far from the Andrea Doria was a British ship. The enmity of the British for Holland, and especially against Statia, was no secret.

"In order to shift the responsibility, Ravené went to consult De Graeff, the governor. De Graeff had already seen the Andrea Doria, for Ravené met him in the streets of the Upper Town. A clever lawyer and a keen business man, the governor had already made up his mind when Ravené spoke.

"'Two guns less than the national salute,'" was the order.

"And, so, the United States was for the first time recognized as a nation by this salute of eleven guns.

"For this act, De Graeff was subsequently recalled to Holland, but he was reinstated as Governor of Statia, and held that position when the island was taken by Rodney in 1781. The Dutch made no apology to England."

Saba, which lies close to Statia, depends for its interest on its location. It is but an old volcanic crater, sticking up out of the sea, in the interior of which a town has been built. As a writer describes it, "if the citizens of this town—which is most fitly called Bottom—wish to look at the sea, they must climb to the rim of the crater, as flies would crawl to the edge of a tea-cup, and look over. They will see the ocean directly below them at the foot of a precipice some 1,300 feet high. To go down to the sea it is necessary to take a path with a slope like the roof of a house, and to descend the Ladder, an appalling stair on the side of a cliff marked at the steepest part by steps cut out of the face of the rock."

This strange town of Bottom is built with a heavy wall all round it, to save it from the torrents which stream down the inside slopes of the crater during a rain. Its population is mainly white, flaxen-haired descendants of the Dutch.

More amazing than all, most of the inhabitants are shipbuilders, but the ships, when built, have to be let down by ropes over the side of the cliff. These fishing smacks are not only built in a crater, but on an island which has neither beach, harbor, landing stage nor safe anchoring ground, where no timber is produced, where no iron is to be found, and where cordage is not made. The island has no more facilities for the shipbuilding trade than a lighthouse on a rock in the middle of the sea.

ABOVE THE HOARSE SHOUTS OF RUFFIANS AND JACK-TARS, ROSE TEACH'S MURDEROUS WAR CRY. ABOVE THE HOARSE SHOUTS OF RUFFIANS AND JACK-TARS, ROSE TEACH'S MURDEROUS WAR CRY.

Passing Saba, the steamer went on to her next port of call, St. Thomas. Here was seen the influence of another European power. Barbados and Trinidad are English; Martinique, French; Statia and Saba, Dutch; but St. Thomas is Danish. It is the chief of the Virgin Islands, and rejoices in a saintlier name than many of its companions which are known as "Rum Island," "Dead Man's Chest," "Drowned Island," "Money Rock," "Cutlass Isle" and so forth, the naming of which shows buccaneer authorship. Even in the town of Charlotte Amalia, the capital of St. Thomas, the stamp of the pirate is strong, for two of the hills above the city are marked by the ruins of old stone buildings, one of which is called "Bluebeard's Castle," and "Blackbeard's Castle," the other. It was once, no doubt, one of the many ports of call of that Nero of pirates, Blackbeard Edward Teach.

Cecil's description of the buccaneers had greatly stimulated Stuart's interest in pirate stories, and, rightly thinking that he could sell a story to his paper by new photographs of "Blackbeard's Castle" and by a retelling of the last fight of that savage scoundrel, he set himself to find out what was known of this career of this "Chiefest and Most Unlovely of all the Pyrates" as he is called in a volume written by one of his contemporaries.

In appearance he was as fierce and repulsive as in character. He was of large size, powerfully built, hairy, with a mane-like beard which, black as his heart, grew up to his very eyes. This beard he twisted into four long tails, tied with ribbons, two of which he tucked behind his outstanding ears, and two over his shoulders. His hair was like a mat and grew low over his forehead. In fact, little of the skin of his face was visible, his fierce eyes glaring from a visage like that of a baboon. In fighting, it was his custom to stick lighted fuses under his hat, the glare of which, reflected in his jet-like eyes, greatly increased the ferocity of his appearance.

Teach was an execrable rascal, who ruled his ship by terror. The worst of his crew admitted him master of horror as well as of men. It was his custom ever and anon to shoot a member of his crew, whenever the fancy pleased him, in order that they should remember that he was captain.

Blackbeard is famous in the annals of piracy for his idea of a pleasant entertainment. One afternoon, when his ship was lying becalmed, the pirates found the time pass heavily. They had polished their weapons till they shone like silver. They had gambled until one-half of the company was swollen with plunder and the other half, penniless and savage. They had fought until there was nothing left to fight about, and it was too hot to sleep.

At this, Teach, hatless and shoeless, and, says his biographer, "a little flushed with drink"—as a man might be who spent most of his waking hours swigging pure rum—stumbled up on deck and made a proposal to his bored companions.

"I'm a better man than any o' you alive, an' I'll be a better man when we all go below. Here's for proving it!"

At which he routed up half a dozen of the most hardened of the crew, kicked them down into the hold, joined them himself and closed the hatches. There in the close, hot hold, smelling of a thousand odors, they set fire to "several pots full of brimstone and other inflammable matters" and did their best to reproduce what they thought to be the atmosphere of the Pit.

One by one, the rest gave in and burst for the comparatively free air of the deck, but Teach's ugly head was the last to come up the hatch, and his pride thereon was inordinate. It was the surest road to the Captain's good favors to remind him of his prowess in that stench-hole on a tropic afternoon.

Teach's death was worthy of his life. Lieutenant Maynard of H. M. S. Pearl learned that Teach was resting in a quiet cove near Okracoke Inlet, not far from Hatteras, N. C. He followed the pirate in a small sloop. Teach ran his craft ashore.

Maynard was determined to get alongside the pirate, so with desperate haste he began to throw his ballast overboard. More than that, he staved in every water cask, until, feeling that he had enough freeboard, he slipped his anchor, set his mainsail and jib, and bore down upon the stranded sea robber.

As he came on, Teach, with fuses glowing under his hat, hailed him, and, standing on the taffrail, defied him and drank to his bloody end in a goblet of rum.... Teach, surrounded by his sullen and villainous gang, shrieked out the chorus of a sea song as the sloop drew near and, when she had drifted close enough, he pelted her deck with grenades.

At this moment, the two vessels touched, whereupon Teach and his crew, with hideous yells, and a great gleam of cutlass blades, leapt upon the sloop's deck. Through the smoke cloud the awful figure of the pirate emerged, making for Maynard. At the same time, the men hidden in the sloop scrambled up from below, and the riot of the fight began.

As Teach and Maynard met, they both fired at each other, point blank. The lieutenant dodged, but the robber was hit in the face, and the blood was soon dripping from his beard, the ends of which were, as usual, tucked up over his ears.

There was no time to fumble with pistols now. So they fought with cutlasses. Teach, spitting the blood from his mouth, swore that he would hack Maynard's soul from his body, but his opponent was too fine an adept with the sword to be easily disposed of. It was a fearful duel, a trial of the robber's immense strength against the officer's deftness.

They chased each other about the deck, stumbling across dead bodies, knocking down snarling men, who, clutched together, were fighting with knives. Ever through the mirk could be seen the pirate's grinning teeth and his evil eyes lighted by the burning and smoking fuses on either side of them, ever above the groans of the wounded and the hoarse shouts of ruffians and jack tars, rose Teach's murderous war cry.

At last, Maynard, defending himself from a terrific blow, had his sword blade broken off at the hilt. Now was the pirate's chance. He aimed a slash at Maynard. The lieutenant put up the remnant of his sword and Teach's blow hacked off his fingers. Had the fight been left to the duel between the two, Maynard had not a second to live. But, just as the pirate's blow fell, one of the navy men brought his cutlass down upon the back of the pirate's neck, half severing it. Teach, too enraged to realize it was his death blow, turned on the man and cut him to the deck.

The current of the fight changed. From all sides the jack tars, who dared not close with the pirate chief, fired pistols at him. The decks were slippery with blood. Still fighting, Teach kicked off his shoes, to get a better hold of the planks. His back was to the bulwarks. Six men were attacking him at once.

Panting horribly, and roaring curses still, Teach, with his dripping cutlass, kept them all at bay. He had received twenty-five wounds, five of which were from bullets. His whole body was red. The half-severed head could not be held straight, but some incredible will power enabled him to twist his chin upwards, so that, to the last, his eyes glared with the fierce joy of battle, and the lips, already stiffening, smiled defiantly.

The six men drew back, aghast that a creature so wounded could still live and move, but Teach drew a pistol and was cocking it, when his eyelids closed slowly, as though he were going to sleep, and he fell back on the railing, dead.

So, in fitting manner, perished the last of the great pirates of the Spanish Main.

The Hungry Shark

"Hyar, sah! Please don' you go t'rowin' nuffin to de sharks, not 'roun' dese waters, anyhow."

"Why?" asked Stuart in return, smiling at the grave face of the negro steward on board the steamer taking him from Porto Rico to Jamaica. His stay at Porto Rico had been brief, for he found a telegram awaiting him from Fergus, bidding him hurry at once to Kingston.

"No, sah," repeated the negro, "dar witch-sharks in dese waters, debbil-sharks, too. Folks do say dem ol' buccaneers, when dey died, was so bad dat eben de Bad Place couldn't take 'em. Now, dey's sharks, a-swimmin' to an' fro, an' lookin' for gol', like dem yar pirates used ter do."

"Oh, come, Sam, you don't believe that!" protested the boy. "What could a shark do with gold, if he had it?"

"Sho's you livin', Sah," came the response, "I done see two gol' rings an' a purse taken out'n the inside of a shark. An' you know how, right in dese hyar waters, a shark swallowed some papers, an' it was the findin' o' dose papers what stopped a lot o' trouble between Great Britain an' the United States, yes, Sah!"

The gift of silver crossing a palm has other powers besides that of inspiring a fortune-teller. It can inspire a story-teller, as well. Stuart, scenting a story which he could send to the paper from Kingston, put half-a-crown where he thought it would do most good, namely, in the steward's palm and heard the strange (and absolutely true and authentic) story of the shark's papers.

"Yes, Sah," he began, "I know jes' how that was, 'cause my gran'pap, he was a porter in de Jamaica Institute, an' when I was a small shaver I used to go wid him in the mornin's when he was sweepin' up, and I used to help him dust de cases. Yes, Sah. Bime by, when I got big enough to read, I got a lot o' my eddication from dose cases, yes, Sah!

"This hyar story begins dis way. On July 3, 1799—I remember de dates persackly—a brig, called de Nancy, lef' Baltimore for Curacao. Her owners were Germans, but 'Merican citizens, yes, Sah. Her cargo was s'posed to be dry goods, provisions an' lumber, but dere was a good deal more aboard her, guns, powder an' what they call contraband, ef you know jes' what that is. I don't rightly."

"I do," agreed Stuart. "Go ahead."

"Well, Sah, dis hyar brig Nancy, havin' stopped at Port-au-Prince, started on down de coast, when, strikin' a heavy blow, she los' her maintopmast. She was makin' for a little island, not far 'way, to make some repairs, when she was captured by H.M.S. Sparrow, a cutter belongin' to H.M.S. Abergavenny, de British flagship stationed at Port Royal. De Sparrow was commanded by Lieutenant Hugh Wylie, and dis hyar Wylie sent her in with anoder prize, a Spanish one, to Port Royal. So, naterally, Wylie brings a suit for salvage against de Nancy, bein' an enemy vessel."

"But where does the shark come in?" queried Stuart, growing impatient.

"Jes' you wait a minute, Sah!" the negro responded, "I bring um in de shark pretty quick. De owners of de Nancy, dey come to court an' show papers that de Nancy never was no 'Merican ship at all, an' dat Lieutenant Wylie, he make one great big mistake in capturin' dis hyar brig.

"But, what you t'ink, Sah? Right at dat moment, up steps in de court-room, Lieutenant Fitton, of H.M.S. Ferret, another cutter belongin' to the Abergavenny an' hands the judge some papers.

"'Your Honor,' he says, 'these are the true papers of the brig Nancy. Those you have before you are false.'

"'Where did you find these papers?' ask de judge.

"'In the belly of a shark, My Lord,' answers Lieutenant Fitton, clear an' loud.

"For de sake, Sah, dem Germans must ha' turn green! In de belly ob a shark, Yah, ha-ha!" And the steward roared in white-toothed laughter.

"But how were they found there?" came the boy's next question.

"Yes, Sah, I was jes' comin' to that. Dis hyar Fitton, wid one cutter, was a-cruisin' together wid Wylie, in de other cutter, when Wylie broke away to take de Nancy.

"Bein' nigh breakfast time, Fitton signals to Wylie to come to breakfast. Wylie, he right busy wid Nancy an' can't come right away. Fitton, fishin' while he waitin' for Wylie, catch a small shark. Dey cut him open, jes' to see what he got inside, an' dar, right smack in de belly, dey see a bundle o' papers.

"'Hi!' says Fitton, 'dat somet'ing important!' and he keep de papers an' tow de shark to Port Royal."

"I suppose," said Stuart, "the captain of the Nancy must have thrown the papers overboard. But why should the shark swallow them? I know sharks will turn over and make ready to swallow most things, but they don't take them in, as a rule, unless they're eatable."

"Yes, Sah, quite right, Sah, but dar was a reason. De papers, Sah, had been hidden in a pork barrel on board de Nancy, an' de shark must ha' t'ought dey smelt good. When Fitton showed dese hyar papers in court, de experts what were called in on de case said dat dere was grease on 'em what wouldn't come from no shark's stomach. No, Sah.

"Dey figured, right den an' dar, dat de grease must ha' been on de papers, fust. So dey started lookin' on board de Nancy an', for de sake, dey found, right in a pork barrel, a lot more papers, all written in German an' showin' a reg'lar plot for privateerin' against the United States.

"Dose papers, Sah, dey're right thar in de Institute in Jamaica, wid a letter from de official, who was in charge ob de case, ober a hundred years ago. In de United Service Museum, in London, is de head of de shark what swallowed de papers. I reckon, Sah, dat was de fust time dat a shark ever was a witness in a court!"

And, with a loud laugh, the steward went to respond to the call of another of the passengers.

Strange as was the story of the shark swallowing the papers and being forced to give them up again, still stranger was the story that Stuart heard from one of the passengers. This tale, equally authentic, was of an occurrence that happened even earlier, in that famous town of Port Royal, which, in the long ago days, was the English buccaneer center, even as Tortugas was the center of the French sea-rovers.

This was the story of Lewis Galdy, a merchant of Port Royal, French-born and a man of substance, who went through one of the most extraordinary experiences that has ever happened to a human being.

He was walking down the narrow street of that buccaneer town, on June 7, 1692, when the whole city and countryside was shaken by a terrific earthquake shock. The earth opened under the merchant's feet and he dropped into the abyss. He lost consciousness, yet, in a semi-comatose state, felt a second great wrenching of the earth, which heaved him upwards. Water roared about his ears, and he was at the point of drowning, when, suddenly, he found himself swimming in the sea, half-a-mile from land.

As the place where he had been walking was fully three hundred yards inland, he had been carried in the bowels of the earth three-quarters of a mile before being thrown forth. A boat picked him up, and he lived for forty-seven years after his extraordinary escape.

Jamaica, indeed, has been the prey of earthquakes, the most serious of which wrecked the city of Kingston, in 1907. The shocks lasted ten seconds, and the town of 46,000 inhabitants was a ruin. The death list reached nearly a thousand. From this shock, however, as Stuart found, the city has recovered bravely, largely due to the lighter system of building common to British islands, and all places which have an American impress, while in French, Dutch and Danish islands, buildings are more solidly constructed. Frame houses, however, are less damaged by earthquake than are stone structures.

There was, however, little opportunity for Stuart to make tours in Jamaica or to work out any articles for his "Color Question" series. A registered letter from the paper awaited the boy in Kingston, the reading of which he concluded with a long, low whistle.

That night, without attracting attention, Stuart left the city on foot, taking neither tramway nor railroad, and made a long night march. The roads were steep, but the cool air compensated for that difficulty, and having spent a long time on board ship the boy was glad to stretch his legs. On the further side of Spanish Town he saw what he sought, a rickety automobile under a lean-to-shed.

He hurried to the negro owner, who was lolling on the verandah.

"I want to go to Buff Bay," he said. "How soon can you get me there?"

"De road ain' none too good, Sah," the Jamaican answered, "your bes' way is to take de train f'm Spanish Town. Dat'll land you right in Buff Bay."

"I don't want to," answered Stuart, making up the first excuse that came to mind, "I get train-sick. Can't your car make it?"

The boy knew that there is nothing in the world that so much touches a man's pride as to have his car slighted, no matter whether it be the craziest kettle on wheels or a powerful racer.

"Make it? Yes, Sah!" The exclamation was emphatic. "I can have you in thar by noon."

Business arrangements were rapidly concluded, and in a few minutes they started out, Stuart having borrowed an old straw hat from the driver, in order, as he said, that he could take a good sleep under it, which indeed, he did. But his main reason was disguise.

The negro looked back at his passenger once or twice, and muttered,

"Train-sick? Huh! Looks more like ter me he's in pickle wid de police! Wonder if I didn't ought to say somet'ing?"

Then a remembrance of some of his own earlier days came to him, and he chuckled.

"Fo' de sake!" he said. "I wouldn' want to tell all I ever did!"

And he drove on through Linfield, without summoning the guardians of the law.

Stuart, unconscious how near he had been to an unpleasant delay, slept on. Questioning would have been awkward, search would have been worse, for, in the pocket of his jacket, was Fergus's letter he had received in Kingston, which closed with the words,

"Get to the Mole St. Nicholas with utmost speed! Spare no expense, but go secretly!"

That this bore some new development in the Great Plot, there was no doubting, and the letter had told him to be sure to leave Kingston without letting Cecil catch a glimpse of him. That meant that Cecil was still in Kingston. In that case, what could the other conspirators be doing without him?

Towards noon, a whiff of salt air wakened Stuart. He stirred, rubbed his eyes and looked round.

"The north shore, eh!" he exclaimed on seeing the sea.

"Yes, Sah! Annotta Bay, Sah!"

"Do you know anyone around these parts?"

"Fo' de sake, yes, Sah! I was born in dese parts. I jes' went to Spanish Town a few years ago, when my wife's folks died."

"Do you know anyone who has a motor boat?"

"You want to buy one?"

"Not unless I have to. Do you happen to know of any?"

"Well, Sah," said the negro cautiously, "thar's a preacher here what has one, but—but—he's a mighty careful man is Brother Fliss, an'—"

Stuart, refreshed from his sleep, grasped the hitch at once.

"You think I'm in trouble and running from the police, eh? Not a bit of it! Here, run up to this preacher's. I'll convince him, in a minute."

A little further on, the machine turned to the left, and just as it turned off, a racing car flashed by. Something about one of the figures was familiar.

"Whose car was that?"

The driver turned and stared at the cloud of dust.

"I didn't rightly see, it might ha' been—" He stopped. "I'll tell you whar you can get a boat, Sah!" he suggested. "Mr. Cecil, he keeps one down at his place a bit down de road."

"Cecil!" Stuart had to control himself to keep from shouting the name. "Has he a place on this coast?"

"Yes, Sah; fine place, Sah, pretty place. Awful nice man, Mr. Cecil. He'll lend you de boat, for nuffin', likely. Brother Fliss, good man, you un'erstand, but he stick close to de money."

"Let's go there, just the same," said Stuart, "I don't want to be under obligations. I'd rather pay my way."

The negro shrugged his shoulders and, in a few minutes, the car stopped at the preacher's house.

As the driver had suggested, Brother Fliss "stick close to de money" and his charge was high. He was an intensely loyal British subject, and an even more loyal Jamaican, and when Stuart showed his card from the paper and at the same suggested that he needed this help in order to trace up a plot against Jamaica, the preacher was so willing that he would almost—but not quite—have lent the boat free.

Being afraid that the automobile driver might talk, if he returned to Spanish Town, and thus overset all the secrecy that Stuart flattered himself he had so far maintained, the boy suggested that the negro come along in the boat. This suggestion was at once accepted, for the mystery of the affair had greatly excited the Jamaican's curiosity.

The preacher, himself, received the suggestion with approval. Usually—for the craft, though, sturdy, was a small one—he was his own steersman and engineer. Now, he could enjoy the luxury of a crew, and the driver, who was a fairly good mechanic, was quite competent to handle the small two-cylinder engine.

So far as the boy was concerned, he had another reason. The quest might be dangerous. Undoubtedly Cesar Leborge and Manuel Polliovo would be there. Equally certainly, Guy Cecil, who had protected him before, would not. A companion would be of aid in a pinch.

And it was all so dark, so mysterious, so incomprehensible! He had learned nothing new about the plot. He had no documents with which to confront the conspirators. He had no protection against these two men, one of whom, he knew, had vowed to kill him.

The motor boat glided out on the waters north of Jamaica, on her way to that grim passage-way between Cuba and Haiti, that key to the Caribbean, which is guarded by the Mole St. Nicholas.

Yet, withal, Stuart had one protector. Behind him stood the power of a New York newspaper, and, with that, he felt he had the power of the United States. There is no flinching, no desertion in the great army of news-gatherers. There should be none in him.

With no support but that, with nothing to guide him but his faith in the paper that sent him forth, Stuart set his face to the shore of that semi-savage land, on the beach of which he expected to find his foes awaiting him.

Trapped!

All that night the little motor boat chugged on. She was small for so long a sea-passage, but the preacher knew her ways well. Many a journey had he taken to the Caymans and other Jamaican possessions in the interests of his faith.

In the night-watches, Stuart grew to have a strong respect for him, for the preacher was one in whom the missionary spirit burned strongly, and he was as sincere as he was simple. Each of the three on board took turns to sleep, leaving two to manage the boat. Stuart got a double dose of sleep, for the preacher, seeing that the boy was tired, ran the craft alone during the second part of his watch.

Dawn found them in the Windward Passage, with the Mole of St. Nicholas on the starboard bow. They slowed down for a wash and a bite of breakfast, and then the preacher, with a manner which showed it to be habitual, offered a morning prayer.

The Mole St. Nicholas, at its southern end, has some small settlements, but Stuart felt sure that it could not be here that he was to land. They cruised along the shore a while, and, on an isolated point, saw an old half-ruined jetty, with four figures standing there. As the boat drew nearer, Stuart recognized them as Manuel Polliovo, Cesar Leborge and two Cacos guerillas, armed with rifles and machetes.

"Are you afraid to follow me?" queried Stuart to the negro who had driven the automobile.

"'Fraid of dem Haiti niggers? No, Sah. I'm a Jamaican!"

This pride of race among certain negroes—not always rightly valued among the whites—had struck Stuart before. Indeed, he had done a special article on the subject during the voyage on the steamer.

Reaching the wharf, Stuart sprang ashore. The Jamaican at once sought to follow him, but the two Cacos tribesmen stepped forward with uplifted machetes. The odds were too great and Stuart's ally fell back.

"It is very kind of you to come and pay us a visit!" mocked Manuel, as Stuart stepped upon the wharf. "We prefer, however, to have you alone. We do not know your guests."

"You know me, then?"

"I knew the ragged horse-boy to be Stuart Garfield, all the way on the road to Millot and the Citadel," the Cuban purred. "I cannot congratulate you on your cleverness. The disguise was very poor."

Stuart thrust forward his chin aggressively, but no retort came to mind.

"I missed you, on the return journey," Manuel continued.

"Yes," the boy answered. "I came down another way."

"Perhaps you borrowed a pair of wings from the Englishman?"

Stuart made no reply.

But this ironic fencing was not to Leborge's taste. He broke in, abruptly,

"You spy on us once, Yes! You spy on us again, Yes! You spy no more, No!"

He made a rough gesture, at which one of the Cacos dashed upon the boy, pinned his arms to his sides and harshly, but deftly, tied him securely with a rope. This done, the Haitian took the boy's small revolver from his pocket and cast it contemptuously on the ground.

"The white carries a pistol, Yes! But he does not even know how to shoot it!"

The phrase irritated Stuart, but he had sense enough to keep still. As a matter of fact, he was a fairly good shot, but, with four to one against him, any attempt at violence would be useless. Besides, Stuart had not lost heart. He had landed, in the very teeth of his foes, confident that Fergus would never have directed him to go to the Mole St. Nicholas, unless the editor had cause. The boy's only cue was to await developments.

At this juncture, the Jamaican preacher, with a good deal of courage, as well as dignity, rose in the boat. He thrust aside, as unimportant, the machete of the Caco who threatened him, and the assumption of authority took the guerilla aback. Quietly, and with perfect coolness, he walked up to the Haitian general. A little to Stuart's surprise, he spoke the Haitian dialect perfectly.

"You're goin' to untie de ropes 'round dat boy, Yes!" he declared, "an' if you're wise, you do it quick. De Good Book say—'Dose who slay by de sword, shall be slain by de sword, demselbes,' Yes! I tell you, dose dat ties oders up, is goin' to be tied up demselbes, Yes!"

"What are you doin' here?" demanded Leborge, with an oath.

"I's a minister ob de gospel," said the preacher, standing his ground without a quaver, in face of the threatening aspect of the giant Haitian, "an' I tell you"—he pointed a finger accusingly—"dat, for ebery oath you make hyar in de face ob de sun, you is goin' to pay, an' pay heabily, before dat sun go down!

"You's a big nigger," the preacher went on, his voice taking the high drone of prophetic utterance, "an' you's all cobered wit' gol' lace. De Good Book say—'Hab no respec' for dem dat wears fine apparel.' No! 'Deir garments shall be mof-eaten, deir gol' an' silver shall be cankered, an' de worm'—hear, you nigger!—'de worm, shall hab 'em'!"

Leborge, superstitious like all the Haitian negroes, cowered before the preacher who advanced on him with shaking finger.

But Manuel was of another stripe.

He strode forward, put a lean but sinewy hand on the preacher's shoulder and twisted him round, with a gesture as though he would hurl him into the water, when there came a sharp,

"Spat!"

The Cuban's hat leaped from his head and fluttered slowly to the ground, a bullet-hole through the crown.

Manuel stared at it, his jaw dropping.

"White man—" the preacher began.

The Cuban took no heed. The shot, he figured, could have come from no one but the negro in the boat, and he wheeled on him, flashing his revolver. As he turned to the sea, however, he saw a motor boat coming at terrific speed into the harbor. He took one glance at it.

"We've got to get rid of the boy before he comes!" he cried.

Leborge, with a wide grin, gave a nod of approval, and Manuel's gun came slowly to the shoulder, for cat-like, he wanted to torture the boy before he fired.

Quicker than his grave manner would have seemed to forecast, the preacher stepped fairly between the Cuban and his victim.

"De Good Book say—" he began, but Manuel gave him a push. There was a slight struggle and a flash.

The preacher fell.

Manuel turned on Stuart, who had tried to catch the falling man, forgetting for the instant that his hands were tied. He stumbled, and the pistol centered on his heart.

Came another,

"Spat!"

A shrill scream rang out. Manuel's gun fell to the ground, suddenly reddened with blood. The Cuban's hand had been shot through.

Clumsily kneeling, Stuart put his ear to the wounded man's heart. It was beating strongly. The bullet seemed to have struck the collar bone and glanced off, stunning the nerves, but not doing serious injury.

For a moment, the four men stood dazed.

Whence came these bullets that made no sound? Could the Englishman be shooting? They stared out to sea.

The "chug-chug" of the motor boat was deafening, now. It stopped, suddenly, and, standing in the bow, the figure of Cecil could be plainly seen. He held no gun in his hand, however.

Never was the Englishman's quiet power more strongly shown than in the fact that, in this tense moment, the conspirators waited till he landed. Leborge shuffled his feet uneasily. Manuel, his face twisted with pain, and holding his wounded arm, glared at his fellow-conspirator, undauntedly.

"My friend," said Cecil to him, calmly, "I have many times instructed you that nothing is to be done until I give the word."

The Cuban cursed, but made no other answer.

"As for you," the Englishman continued, turning to Leborge, "I have told you before that the time to quarrel about the sharing of the spoils was after the spoils were won. Why have you posted men to murder Manuel and me, in the granadilla wood, between here and Cap Haitien?"

The giant would have liked to lie, but Cecil's determined gaze was full on him, and he flinched beneath it, as a wild beast flinches before its tamer.

"If you had waited for me," the calm voice went on, "I might have helped you to escape, but now—"

He raised his hat and passed his hand over his hair, as though the sun had given him a headache.

At the same moment, as though this gesture had been a signal, from the low bushes a hundred yards away burst a squad of a dozen men, rifles at the "ready," in the uniform of American marines.

Manuel and Leborge cast wild glances around, seeking some place to flee, but there was none. They were cut off.

"Quick, Cecil!" they cried, together. And Leborge added, "Your boat! She is fast!"

"Not as fast as a rifle bullet," was the quiet answer.

At the double the Marines came over the scrubby ground, and, running beside the officer in command was a figure that Stuart recognized—his father!

The officer of the Marines came up.

"Seize them!" he said briefly.

The boys in blue disarmed and bound the four, one of the Marines freeing Stuart's arms the while. The second he was free, Stuart sprang forward and grasped his father's hand with a squeeze that made the older man wince.

"Father!" he cried. "It's really you!"

The American official clapped the boy on the shoulder with praise and a look of pride.

"Reckon that high-powered air rifle came in handy, eh?" he answered.

"Was it you, Father, who did the shooting?"

"No, not me. Wish I could shoot like that! We brought along the crack sharp-shooter of the camp."

One of the Marines looked up and grinned.

"This chap," the official continued, "could hit the hind leg of a fly that's scratching himself on a post fifty yards away!"

Then, to Stuart's enormous surprise, he turned to the prisoners with an air of authority.

"In the name of the United States," he said, "you are arrested. You, Cesar Leborge, for having plotted against American authority in Haiti, while holding rank in the Haitian Army; also for having accepted a bribe from other Haitian officials for betraying your fellow-conspirator; also for having given money and issued orders to a band of Cacos to post themselves in ambush with the purpose and intent of murdering Haitian and American citizens.

"You, Manuel Polliovo," he continued, turning to the second prisoner, "are arrested on a Cuban warrant for the murder of one Gonzales Elivo, a guard at the prison from which you escaped two years ago; also upon a charge of assault and attempted murder against this negro minister, for which there are several witnesses present; also on a charge of attempted murder of Stuart Garfield, son of an American citizen; also on a Haitian warrant for conspiring against the peace of the Republic."

Stuart stood with wide-open eyes, watching the dénouement. He stepped back, and waited to see what would be said to Cecil, who, so far, had remained motionless.

The Marines, at a word from their officer, turned to go, taking the prisoners with them.

"And Cecil, Father?" the boy asked, in a low voice.

"Mr. Guy Cecil, my son," replied the American official, "is my very good friend, as well as yours, and the very good friend of the United States. No man knows more of the inner workings of affairs in the West Indies, and he has the confidence of his Government.

"It was through him that I was first advised of this plot to seize the northern peninsula of Haiti, from the Citadel of La Ferrière to the Mole St. Nicholas, to make of this stretch a small republic as was done at Panama, and to sell the Mole St. Nicholas, as a naval base, to a certain European power which is seeking to regain its lost prestige.

"It was a pretty plot, and your investigations, my boy, will help to bring the criminals to judgment.

"Also, I think, Mr. Cecil will release you from your promise not to tell the secret, and you can write your story to the press. It will be a scoop! Only—" he smiled—"don't say too much about the crimes of the arch-conspirator, Guy Cecil!"

"Then he's not a conspirator, at all!" cried Stuart, half-sorry and half-glad.

"Rather, an ally," his father answered, "an ally with me, just as his government is in alliance with our government, an alliance among the English-speaking peoples to keep the peace of the world."